disco inferno!

A
Crosstown Romance
in the
Summer of '79

a novel
Doug E. Jones

RED APPLE
PUBLISHING

Text copyright © 2015 Doug E. Jones
All rights reserved
ISBN: 1514399652
ISBN-13: 978-1514399651

for all our friends back home...

CONTENTS

"People were chanting 'Disco sucks, Disco sucks.' I just picked up on it, playing along, thinking that was the spirit of the night. That was before everything got out of hand. At one point they had me playing 'Take Me Out To The Ball Game.' We tried to pull out all the stops, but there was no way to calm people down."

--Nancy Faust
White Sox Organist

.

Chapter 1

STAYIN' ALIVE

1979. The end of a decade, sure, but also the end of an era, a turbulent time in Chicago when Disco and Rock 'n' Roll dueled to the death. Bobby turned sixteen that year, and in the span of one week his whole life changed. Check that, it *exploded...*

Bobby got banished to the basement in the summer of '79. Plucked from his third floor perch by his parents, he was accused of walking too loud, talking too loud, playing his music too loud; you get the idea, an overall earth-shattering racket. Before he knew it he was half underground in a cave of brick walls and concrete floors with a couple of small windows that Bobby wasn't even sure could open, not to mention a few brave but fidgety mice. Still, he was a short flight of stairs up to the kitchen, which came in handy when he was hungry, his stomach being a bottomless pit in those days.

To cushion the demotion his parents got him a secondhand bumper pool table made by Chicago Coin. Stunk like an ashtray but his dad got a good deal, paying cash for it behind a bar off Howard Street. A few of the guys down there knew his dad too. Bobby thought maybe these were the ones his gram used to go on about, "roughnecks" that could pull off gold pinky rings and a perm, usually some kind of white man 'fro, like the Phillies third baseman or that guitarist for Journey.

Needless to say, there was a minor hiccup about the price of the table, something about a full set of balls. Whether that was *ball busting* or merely a statement of fact, Bobby wasn't sure. He didn't even know his dad went to a bar. And his dad warned him not to say a peep to his mom, pointing at him and raising his voice. But Bobby didn't mind. Bumper pool was fun as shit, drawing kids from all over the neighborhood. On any given night a Hendershot or a Rosenblum would pop by, maybe even a Mundie or two. That bumper pool table probably caused more fights in the basement than floor hockey.

Bobby slept in his dad's dormant tool room. Small but private. Fit the bed. Anything to get away from the furnace. Of course, now that Bobby was surrounded by all those gizmos and gadgets, it made his mind race, like he had to fix something. Or change it. He just had to remember to shut the vents if he got up to anything fishy.

Finally, his crash pad's best feature, and one surely neglected by his parents if they had any hope of wrangling their rambunctious teenage son, were the storm doors; these big wooden ones that opened up to the backyard, to the world. Bobby referred to it fondly as the *escape hatch*.

As a result, he got quite a few lectures from his parents regarding his whereabouts that summer. And even though they occasionally got angry with him, they never got too mad, not until that July, when Bobby didn't give them much of a choice.

That's the problem with being young; you weren't always looking to avoid trouble so much as you were looking to find it, like an itch you couldn't help but scratch--*hard*.

At sixteen, Bobby only knew that he had to be where the action was at, which usually meant connecting the dots between pizza, girls, and disco. Yes, disco. Outside of his dad, and of course Mr. Cub, Ernie Banks, Bobby looked up to one person and one person only... John Travolta.

That's right. The infatuation sprung to life in 1975 with his role as Vinnie Barbarino on *Welcome Back Kotter*. The show was all kids talked about on Thursday nights: "*Up your nose with a rubber hose.*"

Then Travolta does *Saturday Night Fever* in '77 and *Grease* in '78. You see what I'm saying? He was on a roll. THE MAN. There was really no arguing that. And Bobby had a life-size cardboard cutout of Tony Manero that he stole from Laury's records over on Sherman Avenue to prove it.

Well you can tell by the way I use my walk
I'm a woman's man no time to talk
Music loud and women warm
I've been kicked around since I was born

--The Bee Gees

Don't laugh. Bobby was dead serious. But he became distracted in '79. By a girl. And it wasn't Donna Summer. Oh, he knew plenty of girls, only he was never crazy about anyone in particular, like he wanted to hang out after putting the moves on them.

So he was just as interested in hitting up Gigio's for a couple of slices of pepperoni as he was hitting on the girl next door. And then, of course, there was disco. And if you were into disco, you were into dancing.

His dad wanted him to play a sport in high school. And this was it. Dance. Though with Bobby it was never about who he was dancing with so long as she was decent looking, even if she was uncoordinated or had no rhythm.

You see, he was always stoked for the chance to go solo with a few seemingly off-the-cuff moves or a well-timed kick, one that usually ended in a futile but valiant attempt at the splits.

And if the music got a little groovier, maybe some Heatwave, he effortlessly kept in step with the black chicks when they started line dancing. As far as Bobby was concerned, *Ain't no half steppin'...*

On special occasions, like a buddy's birthday or a Saturday night, Bobby would even borrow his dad's three-piece suit; a blue one made of polyester, the good kind his dad told him. He had this black silk shirt too, with the extra wide collar. And platform shoes.

What can I tell you? He was imitating his hero. Travolta started the whole thing with *Fever*, must've been Christmas of '77. And, as Bobby was about to find out less than two years later, Travolta played a part in ending it too.

Summer, hot but breezy, enormous elm trees camouflaging street after street of beautiful old homes along a boundless blue lake. This is where Bobby lives. Evanston, Illinois -- the first suburb north of Chicago along Lake Michigan. For Bobby, the lakefront is an endless playground for goofing off and finding trouble is easy. But today, on the 4th of July, he's on his way to work.

Bobby pedals his Stingray past a string of Victorian homes boasting wrap-around porches draped in ivy. The normal route. But Bobby feels anything but normal seeing as his confidence is being messed with by a tinge of doubt. It's his bike. He thinks maybe he's outgrown it. And not because he's just squeezed past six-foot in the last couple months.

You see, one by one, boys his age around town are starting to drive cars. And a car means everything. Beginning with freedom. So if you have a car, or access to one, say your dad's '75 Mercury station wagon, you can dictate the day so to speak, kind of call the shots with your friends without too much hassle. Like, "Shut up unless you got some gas money."

Make no mistake though, Bobby loves his bike, a 5-speed Schwinn. Has had it going on six summers. It's bright yellow, a Lemon Peeler they call it, with a matching yellow banana seat highlighted by two black racing stripes. Super cool. The Harley of bicycles. Basically, it's his pride and joy. Even more so than his family's Dachshund, the temperamental Heike, whom they've had going on twelve summers.

A closer look at Bobby finds him in a pair of green canvas All Stars, hi-tops with purple laces, no socks, and cut-off jeans, cut fashionably high and fraying quite well for this early in the summer. And he's not wearing a shirt over his broad, bony shoulders, just his work windbreaker, turned inside out to signify that he isn't on duty.

By the time Bobby reaches the end of Clark Street at sunset, the park is mobbed with people; stretching out on blankets, chowing down cheeseburgers, catching up with friends. Despite losing light, there's a 16-inch softball game in one corner and a few overeager parents still trying to organize an egg toss in another, all of them somehow ending up in the middle of a water balloon fight being waged by a pack of screaming, probably drunk, teenagers.

The beach itself is empty, a safety issue, since that's where the city is planning to launch all the fireworks. Evanston always puts on a better than average show. So there's laughter cutting through the heavy, humid air and loud music on suitcase-size boomboxes, even some dancing.

Bobby hops off his bike, forced to walk it along the crowded path. He watches as a man polishes off the last of his Old Style, saving just enough of the beer to extinguish his grill. Farther on, a frantic mother chases after her kids with a can of mosquito repellant, while a couple of pre-teen pyros light a pack of firecrackers in a metal garbage can, *CRACK CRACK CRACK*, frightening a little girl back to her family, still clutching her snow cone.

Figuring it's going to take forever to get to work this way, Bobby cuts across the grass to Sheridan Road and gets on his bike again. His straight brown hair parted neatly in the middle, feathering back just so in the wind, he's picking up speed when someone *honks* him from behind. But Bobby knows he's far enough over to the right and blindly gives the car behind him *the bird* without so much as a glance. A gold '77 Impala, full of teenagers, *honks* him again anyway, pulling along beside him...

A boy, Bobby's age, trippy Yes t-shirt, sticks his head out the passenger side window. "Hey, man," hollers Scooter from somewhere between his mane of sandy blond hair. "Been working on any new dance moves?"

Bobby keeps pedaling but looks over at Scooter. "Really?" he asks, innocently.

"Sure," confirms Scooter with an inviting smile.

Bobby turns his attention back to the road, missing Scooter's smile morph into a smirk. "Actually there's a step I've been practicing," continues Bobby. "It's kind of like dancing backwards if that makes any sense."

"It doesn't."

"Okay, well, I can show you later."

"Bobby, chill. I'm just messing with you."

"Oh." Bobby looks at Scooter again, trying to read him, but the setting sun catches his friend's eyes, so bright and blue they're dangerous. "Never mind."

Fortunately, Scooter plays it straight for a minute, kind of. "I've got bad news for you, Bobby... Disco's dead."

Bobby ignores him, picking up the pace on his bike.

"You hear me, Bobby?" tries Scooter again, following in the car. "Disco. Is. Dead."

"What're you talking about?" asks Bobby, growing irritable. "That doesn't make any sense." He shakes his head in disbelief. "I heard 'Boogie Wonderland' on WLS twenty minutes ago."

Scooter shares a knowing glance with Reggie, who's behind the wheel of the Impala. "Look, Bobby, you know I like the nightlife."

Reggie checks his afro, which has reached new heights this summer, in the rearview mirror. "And I like to boogie."

"But if Steve Dahl pulls off this Disco Demolition thing next week, it's over," explains Scooter. "Not even Gloria Gaynor will survive."

"Or your boy Travolta," adds Reggie.

A blond, Patti, leans out the back window, barely sympathetic. "No one's gonna be doing the hustle anymore, Bobby."

Scooter and Reggie hi-five.

However, Bobby isn't buying it. "Who the hell is Steve Dahl?" he asks, totally annoyed. "I'll kick his ass."

"Take it easy, he's that new deejay on the Loop, the rock station," says Scooter. "People are starting to listen."

"What people?" asks Bobby.

"Half the high school," replies Scooter. "Everybody."

"Really?" Bobby can't believe it. "What about the Rainbo?"

"They'll be playing more Van Halen," replies Patti.

Scooter opens a pouch of Red Man. "And less KC and the Sunshine Band."

"That's not even funny." Bobby turns off Sheridan road, pulling over on a side street, so the Impala can catch up to him and park. "I can't dance to 'Jamie's Cryin'," he tells his friends, "yet alone roller skate."

"That's the cool thing about rock 'n' roll," says Scooter, stowing a wad of tobacco in his mouth. "You don't have to dance, and if you do, you don't have to be good at it."

The other girl in the backseat, Donna, the brown-haired one with a tan to match, finally chimes in, doing so rather sweetly: "I still like to disco, Bobby."

Donna makes Bobby nervous, has since forever. "Uh, thanks, Donna." He places a sneaker back on one of the pedals to signify his imminent departure. "I should get to work."

"Hold on..." Donna gets out of the car in short-shorts, knee-high socks, and a *Jaws* t-shirt; beautiful enough to take her time. She reaches back in for her strawberry Bonne Bell lip gloss, which she puts around her neck on a chain, and then grabs her radio, a Sony AM/FM cassette-corder. "Can I ride with you, Bobby?"

His heart beginning to drum, Bobby wipes the seat clean with his forearm, more gesture than need. "Hop on," he tells her.

"What's up with your bike anyway?" asks Scooter, before Bobby can take off.

"What?" Bobby worriedly scans his Stingray, squeezing both tires. "What do you mean?"

Reggie leans across the seat so he can see Bobby, letting him know he means business. "You were supposed to take your mom's car tonight."

"That was the coast is clear signal." Scooter opens the car door, spitting a stream of tobacco juice on the curb. "So we knew you were the last one out."

"You did get your license this week, didn't you?" asks Reggie.

"Yeah, of course." Bobby anxiously squeezes the handlebars. "It's just that my mom was grilling me so much about her Rabbit, I decided to bike."

Scooter's not impressed. "You're sixteen, dude."

"What does Barbara want from you?" asks Reggie.

Bobby shrugs. "I'm not sure to be honest. And please don't call my mom Barbara."

"That's her name, isn't it?" laughs Reggie.

"Dudes," interrupts Scooter. "This is serious."

"I get that," says Bobby. "The house is empty."

Scooter spits again, most likely for affect, then looks up at him. "It better be."

"It is," Bobby assures them. "Everyone's left to watch the fireworks. Just get the stuff and get out."

"That's cool," says Reggie, "but we were thinking about taking a little more than the weed."

"From my place?" Bobby runs the idea through his head. "Why would you do that?"

"'Cause every time ganja goes missing in Evanston I get grounded for two weeks," complains Scooter.

"And stoned for a month," laughs Patti, shoving Scooter from behind.

"Maybe if we took your sister's stereo," suggests Reggie.

Scooter's on board. "Or the color TV."

Reggie looks around, like he's trying to gather votes. "So none of us get fingered."

"No way. The TV?" Bobby throws his hands up in the air. "How am I supposed to watch the Cubs the rest of the summer?"

"You can watch the games at my house," offers Donna, flashing her hypnotic green eyes.

"Don't do it, Bobby," warns Patti. "Seriously, unless you wanna watch All My Kids, One Life, and GH, her mom won't turn on the Cubs until three."

"That's not true," says Donna, shooting Patti a dirty look as she makes herself comfortable on the back of Bobby's bike. "My mom loves the guy at first base."

"That's Bill Buckner," Bobby tells her.

Donna rests her feet on the back wheel pegs, obligating Bobby to steady the bike and keep her upright. "I think it's his mustache," she says, putting her hands around his waist.

9

Donna's hotness, and something about the way she said *mustache*, catches up to Bobby, making him momentarily light-headed, and he fumbles his words. "Yeah, I mean, well, Buckner's mustache, you know," he starts with her, then snapping out of it, appeals to the rest of them. "I thought the idea was to screw over Debbie's boyfriend, not me."

Growing bored, Patti gets out of the car in her roller skates, a new pair of Chicago Skates she fell in love with and hasn't taken off all summer. "If it's just pot," she says, "Bobby's sister can't tell anyone it's missing... *Duh*."

"She's right," says Bobby, relieved to have someone on his side. "Take anything else and my dad is gonna call the fuzz."

Everyone turns their attention to Scooter, knowing he's had the most experience in this sort of thing. "Sure it's a brick?" he asks.

"It was when Woody first got his hands on it," answers Bobby, "but he's been selling it, quarter ounces, since school got out."

Scooter isn't happy about that. "You're kidding?"

"Don't worry," Bobby tells him. "There's plenty left."

Patti makes herself at home between Bobby's chopper handlebars. "You guys'll be rolling doobies all summer," she says.

"Um... Yeah." Bobby tries to play it cool but he's balancing both girls on his bike now, turning his summer brown cheeks red.

Reggie strokes his chin for guidance. "Suppose we do take just the weed," he wonders, "and we can sell it. How much of the money do you want, Bobby?"

"Yeah, what's your cut?" asks Scooter.

"Nothing," replies Bobby. "I just want Woody out of my sister's life."

"How noble." Scooter spits, barely clearing his chin. "Do you want us to leave an eighth under your mattress?"

"Uh... Nah," says Bobby, pretending to consider it. "Look, I'll catch up with you cats later."

But Reggie isn't done. "Hey, Bobby, 'Boogie Wonderland' isn't disco. That's Earth, Wind & Fire, man. That's R&B."

"I know, I know," concedes Bobby. "But they made a disco record, so did Kiss, and that British guy. What's his name? With the nose."

Patti bails him out. "Rod Stewart."

"Yeah, Rod Stewart," repeats Bobby, as if he's made his point.

"And look what happened to him." Scooter turns up the car radio, planted firmly on the Loop FM 98, playing disc jockey Steve Dahl's parody song of Rod Stewart's "Da Ya Think I'm Sexy?" Dahl and his band, Teenage Radiation, call it, "Do You Think I'm Disco?"

In the intro, Dahl's talking:

What's happening, baby, and how the heck are you? My name is Tony. Would you care to dance? No? Hey, calm down, let me get you another piña colada! I mean, what did we join this exclusive disco club for anyway, you know? I mean, it cost a hundred dollars to join and we're supposed to dance! Don't you like my white 3-piece suit, my gold coke spoon, gold razor blade, and gold Italian snaggle tooth, you know?

Bobby rolls his eyes, uninterested, but deep down he's concerned that a song mocking his lifestyle even exists. Rattled, he tries to make a smooth exit but with the two girls aboard he struggles to pick up speed on the bike and wobbles along rather awkwardly. By the time he levels the ride out, Donna has tuned in the Loop on her radio, back to Dahl. Of course, Bobby doesn't say anything, and the three of them listen to Dahl poke fun at disco as they continue along the lake on Sheridan Road...

Dahl sings the first verse:

> I wear tight pants, I always stuff a sock in
> It always makes the ladies start to talkin'
> My shirt is open, I never use the buttons
> So I look hip, I work for E.F. Hutton

Then Dahl sings the chorus:

> Do you think I'm disco?
> 'Cause I spend so much time
> blow dryin' out my hair
> Do you think I'm disco?
> 'Cause I know the dance steps
> learned them all at Fred Astaire

Bobby stops at Greenwood Beach, where he sees his parents picnicking with neighbors in the park, allowing Patti and Donna to hop off his Stingray... and take the radio and that stupid song with them. Relieved, he walks the bike over to his mom. It's the 4th. She wants a hug and a kiss, but in doing so spots the two girls over his shoulder. "When are you going to ask Donna out?"

"What?" Bobby asks, though he heard her clearly.

"She's so pretty," she continues, quite attractive herself.

Bobby's dad approaches, handing his wife a cocktail. "We were just talking to Donna's parents."

Bobby's stomach begins to knot. "So..."

"You should take her to a movie," his mom tells him, stirring the drink with her finger.

Bobby's dad looks at his wife. "Didn't one of the Mundie girls see *Meatballs?*"

"Mm-hmm," she nods, taking a sip of her drink. "Cathy said Bill Murray was very funny. You know, the one from the TV."

"*Saturday Night Live,*" fills in his dad, scoring brownie points.

"I know who he is," says an exasperated Bobby.

"So take her," she repeats.

"Mom, you've been trying to get me to ask Donna out since the 3rd grade."

"I think that's how long she's had a crush on you," says his dad, hanging his arm around Bobby's shoulder.

"Dad..." Bobby slips out from under his grasp. "We're just friends."

"That's how it starts," he says, winking at his wife. "In fact, I recall your mother being quite friendly when we met."

"Don't be dirty." She acts offended but gives her husband a playful slap on his behind before rejoining their friends...

Bobby's heard and now seen enough but when his mom's out of earshot, his dad moves in, dispensing a little unsolicited advice. "All women want is for someone to pay attention to them."

"Huh?" Bobby backs up, itching to get away, but walks into one of those giant elm trees Evanston is famous for.

His dad, as tall as Bobby but thicker, has him practically pinned against the bark. "Just a hi or your hair looks nice, maybe something goes together, like her shoes and her ... eye shadow."

Bobby humors him. "Okay, dad."

"Trust me," he smiles. "Your mom was a catch, still is."

"I get it. Pay attention to them." Bobby looks around, trying to find something else to talk about, then does. "I don't see Debbie."

"She'll be back in a minute."

Bobby checks the sky. "It's almost dark. I thought she was hanging out with you guys tonight."

"She is," confirms his dad. "Woody forgot his whistle at the house so Debbie went back for it."

"His whistle?"

"There're a lot of people on the lakefront tonight."

Bobby looks back toward home, doing a poor job of masking his concern. "What a dork."

"He's harmless."

"I should go help her, make sure she finds his precious whistle."

Bobby's dad taps his watch. "You were lucky enough to get off work for the parade."

Bobby knows he's right and grabs his bike but dispenses a little knowledge of his own before leaving. "Did you know Debbie's thinking about giving up her scholarship to Berkeley?"

"Why on earth would she do that?" asks his dad, confident his son has a punchline.

However, Bobby isn't joking. "To follow Woody down to Carbondale." He takes off again on his bike, this time with urgency.

"That's not funny," his dad calls out, but Bobby's gone...

Scooter, Reggie, and another kid, Tim, Cub hat covering his new buzz cut, sneak past the Rabbit into Bobby's backyard... But they don't get far before Scooter pauses in front of a towering pine tree and pats Tim on the shoulder. "Let us know if you see anyone coming."

Tim is the meat of this group, set to start at linebacker for the varsity going into his junior year at Loyola. But he's not all muscle, although he's paranoid enough to think he has to prove it. "The only thing I'll be able to see from up there is other trees."

"Why do you have to argue about everything?" asks Scooter.

"I'm not fucking arguing," replies Tim, a vein darting across his forehead. "I'm just ... sayin'."

Reggie can see that Tim's angry at what he perceives to be a menial task and tries a different approach. "Look, man. Your coach doesn't send you after the quarterback on every play, right? All of us don't have to rush. Some of us, namely you, can stay back in coverage. Just in case. Catch my drift?"

Scooter nods his head. "Yeah, play safety on this one."

"Safety," repeats Reggie.

"Fine." Tim frowns and begins to climb the pine, limb by limb, like it's a mere ladder, while Scooter and Reggie slip in the house through the back door off the screen porch. It's not locked. Nothing ever is in Evanston.

Chapter 2

HOT STUFF

Bobby jumps off his bike in the parking lot at Dempster Street and races toward a pay phone, fumbling through his pockets for a couple of coins when none other than Woody, nineteen, pulls up in the Evanston Service Crew van, as if he's found what he's looking for. "What're you doing?" he asks, shaking his head disapprovingly. "I need you on the boat ramp."

"Where's Debbie?" demands Bobby, holding out the phone to him while he inserts a couple of dimes into the slot.

"Debs?" Work is one thing to Woody but bugging his girlfriend's little brother takes precedent. "Oh, we went back to your house ... did it everywhere."

Bobby would love nothing more than to punch him square in the nose, and he would do it too if Woody weren't so annoyingly big. Still, he persists. "So is she still there?"

"Might be." Woody taps a pack of Winston's against the steering wheel. "More importantly, the fireworks are about to start and you're not on the ramp."

"It'll just take a second to call her."

"You can talk to her later." Woody sticks a cigarette between his lips, while he searches for something to light it with.

Bobby caves and does him a solid, tossing Woody a blue

lighter, which Bobby carries, even though he doesn't smoke. You see, it was a gift from Scooter, who promised that "fire" would not only please people but impress them as well.

Woody, on the other hand, lights his cigarette without so much as a thank you. "Your job," he tells him instead, pointing his chin at all the bobbing lights out on the lake, "should I choose not to fire your sorry-ass, is to get those boats on dry land tonight without any fuck-ups."

"I got it but--"

"But nothing," Woody tells him, blowing a cloud of smoke in his face without giving it a second thought. "Your sister can wait." He tosses Bobby's lighter on the dashboard, where it lands next to a whistle. "Now get going."

Scooter and Reggie find Heike half asleep in the kitchen, cooling her long body off on the tiles. She barley blinks as the boys go up the back stairs to the second floor of Bobby's house...

Scooter takes a peek down the hall, spotting a door slightly ajar, just enough to catch a glimpse of a tired blanket falling helplessly over the side of the bed. Scooter looks to his friend, aware of the significance. "I've never been granted access to Debbie's room before."

Reggie pulls him back by the shoulder. "Relax."

But Scooter forges ahead, gently pushing the door the rest of the way open with his foot. "Open. Says. Me..."

Without further delay the two of them walk inside Debbie's bedroom, treating it with the proper respect, like they're stepping into a sacred teenage shrine. At eighteen, Debbie is two years older than them. Not quite a hippy, not yet a punk. A 70's child living in a *Partridge Family* world of paisley wallpaper, shag carpeting, and hanging beads, of rainbows painted on the windows and peacock feathers tucked behind her vanity mirror. A lava lamp sits on top of each stereo speaker, psychedelic globs of orange and purple wax bubbling up to the surface.

Mesmerized, Scooter plops down on a bean bag chair by the window to soak it all in, all that is Debbie, as Reggie unearths her album collection; Frampton, Springsteen, and REO Speedwagon, while Jackson Browne waits for his chance on the turntable, one of those new ones with the see-through lid. But the main attraction in Debbie's room has to be the poster of pop star Andy Gibb in tight pink pants and a matching vest, with his shirt open to his belly button.

"His chest is so fucking hairy," says Scooter. "Creeps me out."

Reggie looks up at the ceiling where Andy's poster is practically straddling Debbie's bed. "Think Bobby ever comes in here for a little *shadow dancing* with the brother Gibb?"

You know he loves to dance," laughs Scooter. "He probably can't help himself."

"Look what I found?" Reggie holds up a red bikini top between his thumb and forefinger, unsure if he should even be touching it.

Scooter snatches the top from Reggie. "Stay out of her drawers."

"It was on her bed."

"Really?" Scooter holds the top to his face, breathing in deeply. "Smells like Lake Michigan and Coppertone and ... *sweat*."

"Easy, chief."

"I think I've got a souvenir," smiles Scooter.

"No way. Souvenir's the weed."

"Dude--"

"Don't *dude* me."

"Sorry, dude, I mean, come on, Debbie is a legend. She had boobs in 7th grade, good ones."

"Put. It. Down."

Scooter relents, tossing the top back on the bed. "Bobby said to start with her closet."

"I'm on it." Reggie parts a string of beads and turns on the closet light.

But before he can look around, Scooter stops him. "You hear that?"

Curious, Reggie follows the sound over to the window and sticks his head outside, taking in the fireworks crashing over the lake just a few blocks away. "It's the 4th of July. I get it."

"Nuh-uh." Scooter puts his finger to his mouth, whispering, "Listen..."

And this time, waiting for it, Reggie discerns the sound of running water underneath all the noise outside. He turns to Scooter, worried. "You think someone's here?"

Above the lake, the once black sky is colored with exploding lights, while in the park, homemade quilts and beach blankets consume just about every available inch of grass. Time to sit back and relax, take a load off. However, Bobby's mom is drinking too much. And his dad's surely eating too much, which made the co-ed football with some old classmates a bad idea for both of them, especially when a former girlfriend of his dad's tackled him in the endzone--after he'd already scored.

Bobby's mom is on her last nerve, but she finds Patti and Donna a couple of towels to sit on. The two girls thank her and lay down, side-by-side, arms behind their heads, watching the fireworks.

"That was nice of her," says Donna.

"Yeah."

"She's cool."

"I've never thought about it but, yeah, sure."

"Do you think she likes me?"

"Who're we talking about?" asks Patti.

"Bobby's mom."

"Barbara?"

"Shut-up." Donna playfully smacks her friend's hand. "She'll hear you."

"It's Bobby, isn't?"

"Huh? Where'd that come from?"

"Is that a yes?"

"That's a maybe."

"Now I get the whole Cubs thing. Oh man, this is going to be like 7th grade all over again."

"No," laughs Donna, nervously. "It's not."

Patti mocks her. "*I like to disco, Bobby.*"

"Really?" Donna asks, trying to deflect Patti's point. "Is that what my voice sounds like?"

Back at Bobby's house Reggie is on his hands and knees, quickly but quietly rummaging through Debbie's closet; shoes and shoe-boxes, jackets and jeans. He even checks inside a couple of board games, including, he thinks is clever, *Clue.* But he's coming up empty.

Next, he reaches into the back, behind her retired stuffed animals, and pulls out her ice skates, trying too hard in his opinion to look like they haven't been up to anything this summer. He sticks his hand inside one of them, nothing. Still, he gives the second one a try when, hold on, he digs out a brown sandwich bag, full of something, twisted closed to keep it from spilling or worse when it's in hiding, smelling.

Reggie opens the bag, taking a peek. "Hell, yeah." He looks over his shoulder to share the good news with Scooter, but his friend is gone. So Reggie heads back out into the hallway, where he finds him, just standing there. "I found the shit," he tells Scooter with a big grin. "Let's boogie."

However, Scooter is preoccupied with something. "Hold on." He nods toward the bathroom. "The running water."

"Say what?"

"Look." Scooter shows him that even though the bathroom door isn't open much, there's a straight shot to the mirror over the sink, which by the grace of god is angled perfectly at a steamy shower door, barely concealing a curvaceous female figure, arms above her head, washing her hair, and more importantly, oblivious to her over-stimulated male teen audience.

Reggie's in awe. "It's... Debbie."

"No shit, Sherlock."

"Keep your voice down."

Scooter thinks Reggie wants to stay a while. "Sorry."

He doesn't. "We should get outta here."

"Wait..." Scooter can't take his eyes off Debbie. "You can kind of sort of see her tits through the mist."

Reggie has another look. "Is that a nipple?"

"I'm not sure."

"You're not sure what a nipple looks like?"

"Dude, 8th grade trip. We met some chicks at the Lincoln Memorial. Said they were from New Hampshire or some weird shit. Anyway, we got them to flash us outside the bathrooms."

"I've heard the rest of that story," says Reggie, shaking his head. "Man, you had some weird cats up at Nichols."

"No kidding. That's why I hang out with you dudes. Because you do normal shit."

"Just so you know, Scooter, this ain't normal." Reggie points down the hall. "Come on."

"Dang, it's just getting interesting."

"Doesn't matter, we're leaving."

"Wanna bet?"

Before Reggie can stop him, Scooter darts into the bathroom without Debbie noticing and snatches her bath towel from on top of the sink. A great achievement, yes, but Reggie punches him hard in the arm anyway when he runs back out into the hallway. "What's wrong with you?"

"We'll just hide somewhere until she has to come out."

"You're crazy."

Suddenly, the phone *rings...* and *rings...* and keeps *ringing...*

Reggie and Scooter freeze. Look at each other. Scooter's excited, but Reggie isn't messing around. And the phone? It's still *ringing...*

Heike comes upstairs, surely wondering why no one's picking the phone up when she's trying to nap. She barks twice at the boys, once for each of them.

A vision flashes before Reggie's eyes. It's his mother. She's upset, waving a disapproving finger at him. He grabs Scooter, steering him toward the stairs.

"What?" protests Scooter. "She'll have to come out now."

"And when she does," Reggie tells him, "we can't be here."

Bobby is in the boathouse office on the other end of that phone call, desperately trying to warn his friends to get out of his house. He figures if Debbie hasn't made it down to the lake yet, there's a chance she might still be at home. And if she finds Scooter and Reggie there, his summer, perhaps his entire life, is essentially over. But nobody's picking up the phone...

Scooter and Reggie fly out the back door with the weed, and Debbie's towel, stopping only to get Tim out of the tree. However, their buddy's not budging.

"Why the fuck not?" Scooter asks him.

Tim looks down at his friends, totally serious. "Because *mine eyes have seen the glory.*"

Scooter and Reggie realize right away that Tim must have a bird's eye view of the second floor and start climbing the tree for a better look, just in time to catch a shot of Debbie in the bathroom window, naked and soaking wet, hopelessly looking for her towel.

The stars have aligned. The curtain has been lifted. The boys can't believe their good fortune. Seriously, this happens maybe once in a lifetime. And Debbie's a total babe.

The boys let out a collective groan when she leaves the bathroom, out of their line of vision, followed by a sigh of relief when she emerges in her bedroom, flanked by the two lava lamps like she's in an exotic beauty pageant.

The boys find a couple of good branches to sit on with a decent view. "Can you believe this?" Tim asks them.

"Not really," admits Reggie.

"Dudes," starts Scooter. "I think I know what I wanna do when I grow up."

"Here we go," says Reggie, shaking his head.

"I want to be a bra," continues Scooter, already a million miles away with Debbie, "so I can offer support."

"Nice one," laughs Tim.

"What do you think?" asks Reggie, staring at Debbie. "C-cups?"

"More like Stanley Cups," replies Tim.

"Who's Stanley?" asks Reggie. "I thought she was dating Woody."

"Forget it," says Tim, pointing past Reggie to Scooter. "You guys said to let you know if I saw anyone coming."

Reggie looks over at Scooter, who, transfixed by Debbie, has his hand down his pants. "Don't be such a spaz." He breaks off a pine cone and throws it at Scooter, hitting him in the head.

Scooter quickly pulls his hand out of his pants as if it was nothing. "I was scratching my balls, just for a second, that's all," explains Scooter, though his friends aren't sure whether to believe him or not.

Unfortunately, by the time the boys turn their attention back to Debbie, she's put on a bathrobe and picked up the phone. Show's over. Without speaking, the three of them climb down the tree and scramble out the backyard...

Meanwhile, Debbie's irked to be on the phone. "This better be good, Bobby, I was in the shower."

"You're, uh, missing the fireworks."

"I made some of my own at home."

"That's gross."

"What do you want?"

"Nothing. Just wondering why you weren't with mom and dad."

"I'm eighteen, Bobby."

Bobby's relieved. He doesn't need to one up her. Scooter and Reggie would back off if they heard her on the phone. "You're right, Debs. Sorry." Bobby starts to hang up...

But Woody, already mad about something, grabs the phone out of his hand and slams it down for him. "That nut-job on the ramp."

"Who? What?" Bobby looks toward the water, lit up by a burst of sparkling lights. "That guy? The one who's yelling?"

"Yelling. Swearing. Slurring. Point is," explains Woody, "the jerk doesn't have a permit."

"Why me?"

"Because you work here."

Bobby knows Woody's right, that he has a job to do. Sometimes though, it's hard for him to distinguish between the Woody who is his sister's boyfriend and the Woody who is his boss and whether both of those roles come with too much baggage. So Bobby, having possibly just robbed him of a good amount of weed, gives Woody the benefit of the doubt and hustles back down to the boat ramp...

With the fireworks still blasting overhead, this greasy guy in a once white wife-beater is trying to tie up to the breakwall in a putt-putt, a rowboat with a pint-sized outboard motor on the back; the type of boat you use to get to your real boat.

Bobby runs down the ramp until he's waist-deep in the water. "You can't tie up to the breakwall," he yells out to him.

"I asked her to go over the side," he all but laughs, "and she told me to go fuck myself." He tosses Bobby the front line, daring him not to catch it.

Bobby, of course, grabs the rope but doesn't tie the boat up. Still, what could he do? A girl, his age, stands in the bow, all red hair, freckled legs, and black eyeliner. And she's anxious to get off.

"Do you mind?" she asks, bothered that she has to.

"Uh, no." Bobby's curious and confused, and he just stares at her as the fireworks reach a final crescendo above them before he sticks his hand out to assist her.

However, she ignores him and jumps off the boat, stumbling awkwardly in the shallow water and getting wet.

Bobby starts toward her to help but she makes a beeline past him to the boathouse without so much as a glance, leaving Bobby with little alternative but to hash things out with the guy in the boat. "If you don't have a city of Evanston permit, you can't dock here."

"Do you mind if I wait for my daughter?" He cracks open a can of Miller, which you could do on the lake, kind of, but not on the breakwall.

Bobby looks around. The fireworks have ended. The park is emptying. And boaters are already lining up behind the putt-putt, anxious to go home. "Sir." Bobby clears his throat. "You're blocking the other boats."

"Fuck you." He takes a big chug of beer, too big, and has to wipe his chin with a forearm riddled in faded tattoos.

Bobby decides to make sure the girl finds the bathrooms, less as a courtesy, more to get away from her dad. But as soon as he starts after her, a boy, a couple years older than him and rough around the edges to say the least, beats him to it, jumping out from underneath a tarp on the boat and chasing after her toward the boathouse.

Bobby takes him for her boyfriend and, once again, directs his attention to the lingering putt-putt problem on the boat ramp. "I'm sorry, but you're gonna have to move."

"Fuck off," he barks. The guy's close to forty, needs to shave, probably shower. And he's definitely wasted. "It's goddamn Independence Day. Do you think I need some little prick telling me what to do with my boat?"

"I get it. It's just... Is your trailer parked here?"

"Trailer?" He drinks the rest of his beer. "You think I live in a trailer?" he asks, tossing the can in the lake.

Finding it hard to ignore the blatant litter-bugging, Bobby clarifies himself. "Boat trailer. Did you launch here in Evanston?"

"Hell no."

The wind is kicking up and it's getting choppy, causing several impatient boaters to blast their horns, more than ready to call it a night if it weren't for this troublemaker blocking the ramp.

Bobby tries to remain calm, but Mr. Thomas has let one of his boys swim in to shore for their trailer; the idea being that if the line wasn't forming on the lake, maybe it could in the parking lot. However, it isn't playing out so smoothly, with most of the blame being pinned on Bobby.

"Got people coming over back at the house," Mr. Thomas tells him.

"I understand," sympathizes Bobby.

"Can't you do something about this?" shouts a woman, a pesky kid hanging on her hip, "I need to get the little one to bed."

"Bobby," intervenes her husband, "You either get that guy to move his boat or I'm gonna go around him, rest what may."

"Hold on," pleads Bobby. He knows the guy's serious. He teaches P.E. at the high school. Bobby digs through his dufflebag, removing an old blow horn. He smacks the side of it to make sure the batteries are awake and turns it on, so that his instructions can be heard loud and clear.

Bobby starts with the boaters from Evanston: "Let's line up along the breakwall," he says into the blow horn. "One at a time. We can do this." Then he eyeballs the nut-job, the girl and boy nowhere in sight. "You need to move your boat immediately. You can swing back for them in just a bit."

Bobby turns to the fan of trailers waiting to maneuver down the ramp. "I'll let you know when it's your turn." Bobby checks the order in the water. "Okay, Mr. Thomas," he continues into the blow horn, "tell Steve he can back your trailer up. You guys are first."

Realizing the odds are stacked against him, the guy in the putt-putt relents and takes off, almost clipping the end of the breakwall as he heads south toward Navy Pier.

Woody finally walks over, not to lend a hand but to observe, even though it's obvious Bobby could use help. But Woody's got his clipboard out, pretending to take notes, not that anybody would care to read them.

Eventually, things settle down and Bobby is getting boats out of the water in a timely and efficient manner when an angry girl's voice catches his attention over his shoulder.

"You told my dad to leave?"

Bobby turns around to find the girl from the putt-putt, and she's pissed, her clothes soaked through. "Sorry," mutters Bobby. "He had to, uh, I told him to come back."

"He won't."

"Then how're you getting home?"

"What do you care?"

"I, uh..." Bobby is caught off guard by the directness of her questions, and, more alarmingly, by how damn fine she is. "I, uh, guess I don't know."

"That's what I thought."

"Hold on a sec," says Bobby, trying to do the right thing. "I'm sure I can find you something dry to wear in the boathouse."

She starts to protest but not wanting to drudge around in wet clothes all night, she bites her lip instead.

The lakefront emptied pretty quickly after Bobby got the last boat out of the water. And the rest of the Service Crew helped him get the Whaler on its trailer and back in the boathouse for the night. Meanwhile, Woody added the day's receipts, inaccurately, and closed the register, then gave Bobby the keys when Debbie swung by and reminded him for the third time to lock up—-after he swept the ramp.

All alone, Bobby half-heartedly looks for a broom when the redheaded girl finally emerges from the boathouse in an official *Evanston Lakefront Service Crew* jacket and matching green work shorts. The jacket is definitely big on her, thinks Bobby, but somehow makes her look hot to the point of distraction.

"You, uh, look good in uniform," stumbles out of his mouth without much input from his brain. "Not that I know what you look like out of uniform."

"What?" she asks, placing her wet things in a grocery bag she found inside.

"Nothing. You're dry." He doesn't mean to, but he catches himself staring into her beaming brown eyes. "Uh, that's all that matters."

"Thanks, but I'm not sure I can get away with wearing an Evanston jacket on the South Side."

"South Side?" Bobby asks, a bit confused. "Like over by Mount Trashmore?"

"No," she replies, not sure if a mountain by such an odd name even exists. "The South Side of Chicago. You know, like Leroy Brown."

"As is in *baddest man in the whole damned town*?"

"Something like that," she says, smiling with an ease he hadn't noticed before.

Bobby's interested, not to mention infatuated. "South Side?" he continues, loosening up a bit, so much so he almost sticks his foot in it. "I've never met a... You're a Sox fan?"

"Who else would we root for?"

Baseball talk has Bobby feeling bold. "Kingman, Buckner, the Cubs. Who do the Sox have besides Chet Lemon?"

"Only the best announcer in the world."

"Harry Caray? He could never be the Cubs announcer. He totally rambles."

"Try getting some lights," she says, playfully. "Or do the Cubbies have a bedtime?"

"Baseball was invented in the daytime," reasons Bobby, confidently. "It's part of the game. Its history. Why change now?"

"You've heard of money, right?"

Bobby holds up the keys. "I'm working at this very moment."

"Okay, so how come when other teams are buying championships, you guys are selling? You had to trade Madlock because you weren't going to pay him. You couldn't. Because you can't fill a ballpark during the day when the team's having a down year or it's 97 degrees out or school's in session. Not everybody can skip work to go to a baseball game. Put some lights up and play at night. You'll sell more tickets. And sell more shit. Make more money. Buy better players. Win."

"Not bad," admits Bobby, thinking he should write that down.

"Men spend money," she continues, "not a bunch of boys from the suburbs taking the 'L' into the city to see their first baseball game and drink pops."

Bobby smiles, exaggerating. "I've paid for my fair share of Old Styles at Wrigley."

"Yeah, right, whatever you say."

He reaches out to shake her hand. "I'm Bobby."

"Misty," she says, looking past him. "Not that I'm ever going to see you again."

"Wait. What?" Bobby tries to keep up as she runs down the ramp to greet her dad's boat. "I'm gonna be a junior at Evanston. Where do you live?"

"Bridgeport."

"Bridgeport? Where's Bridgeport?"

Her dad looks up. "Are you shitting me, boy?"

"Ignore him," says Misty. "Mayor Daley was from Bridgeport, Bilandic too."

Bobby's impressed. "Cool."

But her dad is ready to go. "Get in," he says, giving Bobby a dirty look.

Misty turns to Bobby. "Thanks again for the clothes."

"No problem," he says, holding out his hand to help her into the boat.

And this time she takes him up on it. "Thank you."

Bobby smiles. "Any time."

Her dad rolls his eyes and yanks the cord several times to start the motor up again. "Just so you know," he says, pointing at

Bobby, "I don't like you."

"Hey, aren't you missing someone?" Bobby asks, dying to know more. "Your boyfriend?"

Misty scrunches up her nose. "My boyfriend?"

"Yeah."

"Oh, Ian can find his own way back," she says. "He always does."

"I'll turn you around." Bobby grabs ahold of the bow and spins the putt-putt out toward the lake.

"Hold on," says Misty, rummaging through the bag with her stuff. "I think left my Ramones t-shirt in the bathroom."

"I'll get it." Bobby promptly heads for the boathouse but then stops, thinking, and looks back. "Ramones?"

Impatient, her dad takes off, leaving Bobby to watch as Misty disappears into the night over Lake Michigan...

Bummed, Bobby turns back to the boathouse to see Scooter, along with Reggie, Tim, and Donna, lounging about the Impala at the top of the ramp, while Patti practices a barrel roll, spinning in a circle on her skates like a summertime Dorothy Hamill.

"Ramones?" Scooter sits up, spitting a trail of tobacco juice over the edge of the hood. "If you weren't so worried about whether Andy Gibb was gonna join the Bee Gees or not you'd know who the fucking Ramones are, dude."

"I know who they are," lies Bobby. "I just didn't know she liked rock."

"They're punk," clarifies Scooter.

Patti starts singing, *"Twenty twenty twenty four hours to go, I wanna be sedated."*

"They've got a movie coming out in August," adds Tim.

"How am I supposed to know all that?" asks Bobby.

"Look," says Scooter. "If you wanna get down that girl's pants you better give them a listen."

"What? Her?" shrugs off Bobby. "It's not like that."

"Since when?" asks Tim.

"Since--" Bobby steers them to the point. "Tell me you guys are stoned."

Reggie can't help himself, breaking into a big wide grin. "Yup."

"Which means you didn't get caught," hopes Bobby.

Reggie holds up the bag of weed. "Obviously."

"But someone phoned the house while we were inside," says Scooter, "and your sister almost busted us."

Bobby begins lowering the American flag at the top of the ramp. "That was me warning you that she might be home."

"That part we already knew," says Tim.

"So no problems?" asks Bobby.

"Define problem." Reggie holds up Debbie's towel. "I think we saw your sister naked."

"Naked as a jaybird," adds Tim, trying not to laugh as he helps Bobby fold the flag, not the right way but close.

Confused, Bobby takes the towel from Reggie. "What do you mean you think you saw her naked?"

"Well does Debbie have tits like Cheryl Tiegs?" asks Tim.

"Only without the fishnet?" distinguishes Scooter.

Bobby smiles, hoping he's on to them. "Are you guys messing with me?"

Reggie starts up the Impala. "Hop in. We'll explain everything."

Donna hangs back with Bobby while he locks up the boathouse for the night. "We're gonna see *Moonraker* at the Varsity."

"I'll meet you guys," Bobby tells her. "I don't want to leave my bike down here overnight."

But Donna has other ideas. "I'll ride with you."

"Uh, sure, if you want." Bobby looks around. "Just let me grab my... Where the fuck is my bike?" Panic sets in but he tries not to show it. Instead he scans the beach, the boathouse, the ramp, all to no avail before running over to the Impala. "I must've forgot to lock my bike up when I got down here. *Fuck.*"

Patti suggests that, "Maybe someone put it in the boathouse."

Bobby unlocks the boathouse and goes inside but only comes out with Misty's black Ramones t-shirt. He's totally upset. "*Fuck. That dick-wad on the boat.*"

"What dick-wad?" asks Tim.

"The girl in the boat," replies Bobby. "She was with some ... some jerk. I bet he took my bike."

"So what're we waiting for?" wonders Reggie.

"Yeah," says Scooter, sitting shotgun in the car. "Let's go after him."

"It's too late. He's long gone. They're from Chicago," gripes Bobby. "The South Side."

"I've never been past the Shedd Aquarium," says Donna.

Tim pats Bobby on the back and gets in the backseat. "We've got season tickets to the Hawks, but I suppose that's the West Side."

Patti slides in next to Tim. "The South Side might as well be another planet."

"Another planet, another day." Reggie revs the engine. "But tonight, we see Bond."

Donna and Bobby squeeze into the backseat of the Impala, Donna making sure she ends up next to Bobby, who's utterly distraught.

"Don't worry," Donna tells him, whispering into his ear. "You'll get your bike back."

Chapter 3

LET'S GO!

Already in a sweat from the sizzling July heat, Bobby wakes up the next day to the roar of a lawnmower, his lawnmower, the one he's supposed to be cutting the grass with. Annoyed, he sits up in bed, taking a moment to properly rub his groggy eyes, and wraps a sheet around his waist. Then he drags himself over to the storm doors, greeting the cutout of Travolta along the way with a knowing glance, as if both of them had a rough night.

Bobby pushes the wooden doors apart and gingerly walks up a couple of steps, poking his head into the punishing sunlight, one even the elm trees can't obscure. Here, he finds his dad, just standing there in the yard, hot and bothered, with the lawnmower *running*. "Dad! Hello! Hey!"

His dad shuts the mower down and removes his Bears hat, making a point of wiping his shiny forehead with the back of his arm. "Look who's up."

"I said I'd cut the grass."

"When?"

"Today."

"Well..." His dad goes through the motion of checking his watch, even though he's not wearing it. "It's been today for quite some time now."

"Dad, my bike got stolen last night."

He puts his hat back on, low and tight, to keep his face out of the sun. "I heard," he says, "when you and your friends woke me up at two in the morning."

"Sorry."

"Just keep them in the basement next time."

"Everyone was hungry," explains Bobby. "And the girls had to use the bathroom."

"Ahh..." His dad changes his tune. "Did you follow any of my advice? You know, with Donna?"

"Dad, I'm in mourning."

"Or did someone beat you to it?"

"I liked you better when you were mad at me."

His dad lets up. "Do your chores, without me having to ask you, and we can talk about getting you a new bike before the end of the summer."

"Dad," groans Bobby, lowering his head, "the Stingray, it's irreplaceable."

"As far as that model, yes, I'm sorry, forget it."

"It's more than that though," says Bobby. "It'd be like, like trying to replace mom."

His dad looks over his shoulder, making sure the coast is clear. "What if we could replace mom with that new girl on *Charlie's Angels*? Farrah's sister."

"Dad."

"I'm joking."

"That's it? A joke? Grampa gave me that bike. For Christmas."

"Stinks, I know, but it's just a bicycle. You'll get over it."

Bobby's heard enough and goes back down into the basement, his dad failing to dose out the right amount of sympathy. He plops down on his bed and sticks a pillow between his knees, fully prepared to sleep the day away, when the stupid lawnmower kicks up again. His fate sealed, he throws on a pair of gym shorts and heads back out to the yard, snatching the key from the Toro's ignition, much to his dad's amusement.

"First, I need something to eat," Bobby tells him.

"Fine, you have a guest anyway."

"Who?"

"At least I think that's what he is."

Bobby is surprised to find Scooter eating a bowl of Froot Loops at the kitchen table, his hair so long that when he leans over the cereal for a bite, the entire bowl is lost. Kind of cool, thinks Bobby, but he's not alone. Laying at his feet is Heike, silently praying for an errant Fruit Loop, while Bobby's mom, in just her bathrobe, puffs away on a Pall Mall like it's an oxygen tank over by the sink. The three of them, together, isn't what Bobby was expecting, and he's a little more than apprehensive as he takes a seat opposite Scooter at the table.

"What, if you don't mind me asking, are you doing here, Scooter?"

"She had a friend over," he replies, like it was any old excuse. "I thought it'd be okay to sleep on your couch."

"Uh, yeah, the couch. Why not?"

"She's not my real mom," explains Scooter. "She was my dad's second wife."

"Pop-Tarts?" asks Bobby's mom, stuffing a couple in the toaster, the Pall Mall holding on for dear life between her lips. "You're welcome here any time, Scooter."

Scooter tucks his hair behind his ears. "Thanks."

She takes a deep drag on her cigarette and walks over to Bobby. "Scooter told me about your bike," she says, massaging his shoulders.

Bobby buries his head in his hands. "I'm never gonna see my Stingray again."

"Unless," says Scooter, "that Chicago chick's boyfriend has it."

Bobby looks up. "How do you know that was her boyfriend?"

Scooter squints, confused. "'Cause that's what you told us."

"I read in the paper," says Bobby's mom, "that Chicago kids, can you believe this? Kids. Your age. They take the 'L' to the suburbs and then ransack garages. Wilmette. Winnetka. Kenilworth. Even here in Evanston. They'll steal your bike out of the garage and whatever they can stuff in a backpack and then ride to the city like they're coming home from camp."

"Only this one came down on a boat," says Scooter, before turning his attention back to Bobby. "You said the girl was from Bridgeport, right?"

"I think so," says Bobby. "She said Mayor Daley was from there."

Scooter gets up, pours himself a coffee, which Bobby's never seen him do before. "I made some phone calls, looked at a map. Bridgeport, that's where the Sox play."

"Your dad drove Debbie down to Comiskey for a concert," adds Bobby's mom. "What was it? Aerosmith? I'm sure he can give you directions."

"Don't I have to work this afternoon?" asks Bobby.

She turns to the chalkboard by the back door. "Says you're off."

Bobby throws his hands up in the air in disbelief. "You're telling me that I, your one and only son, heir to the throne, apple of your eye, can go all the way to the South Side of Chicago for my bike?"

"Not on your life, but your dad might if you think you know who has it," she says. "Just out of principle."

"We could ask some questions around the neighborhood," suggests Scooter, pouring a stream of sugar in his coffee. "Find the idiot that stole your Stingray."

"And get killed in the city?" Bobby reaches for the Froot Loops. "No way."

A clang, a clatter, and a thud comes from the second floor above their heads. It's Debbie. And she isn't happy. "Bobby!" she yells at the top of her lungs. "Get your ass upstairs!"

Heike runs up the back stairs barking, anxious to see what all the fuss is about, a step slow in her advanced years but just as noisy.

"Or," says Scooter, "you could just get killed here."

Bobby steers the boys south along the lake with an air of trepidation, unsure of how he even got his dad's stationwagon for such a huge task. It's like his parents want to get rid of him, thinks Bobby. After all, the plan to recover his bike means going deep into Chicago. To the other side. The wrong side. The South Side.

Adding to Bobby's anxiety is that North Side legends have failed before him on the South Side. In '74, the Cubs sent Ron Santo across town for a final forgettable season with the White Sox. While in '78, another Cub, Don Kessinger, became Sox manager in addition to his starting shortstop duties, without much success at either.

Even so, all that's easily forgotten by the time Bobby hits 60 mph down Lake Shore Drive; the Drake Hotel, the Playboy sign, and the Hancock building rapidly coming into view, getting bigger and bigger, as if springing to life.

Scooter sits shotgun, like he seems to do for everyone, while Reggie's got the backseat to himself. And he's taking advantage of it too, stretching out for a nap. Tim, the biggest of the four, is in the way back, which he doesn't mind seeing as he enjoys talking to strangers out the rear window like they're long lost relatives.

Meanwhile, Scooter's got the radio dialed in to the Loop, where that Dahl character is spouting off again, much to Bobby's annoyance:

```
"There are kids in India who want
Bee Gees records, I know, I've
seen it. Sally Struthers talks
about it. Send your Bee Gees
records to India."
```

Bobby slaps the steering wheel. "What does Dahl want from me?"

"Your soul," says Scooter, grinning.

"Come on, why's he so down on disco?" wonders Bobby.

"Maybe he can't dance?" proposes Reggie, his eyes still shut.

"I know I can't," admits Tim. "My aunt thinks I've got two left feet."

Reggie sits up. "You say that like it's a real thing."

"I don't know," starts Tim. "I mean, chasing after some kid from Fenwick with a football under his arm is smooth sailing... But trying to shake my groove thing at the 'Y' just isn't happening for me."

"Thanks for sharing," jokes Scooter.

"Like you can do any better." Tim throws a nerf football the length of the stationwagon, narrowly missing Scooter's head.

"Guys," pleads Bobby. "No messing around in the car."

"Sorry," apologizes Tim.

"If you want to learn to dance, Tim, I can help you out," offers Bobby. "We'll start with some stretching."

"Stretching?" asks Scooter. "Are you fucking serious?"

"Maybe Bobby's right," says Reggie, trying not to laugh. "Maybe dancing should be a sport at the high school."

The boys laugh at Bobby's expense until their attention turns back to Dahl on the radio:

```
"You know what? Ethel
Merman has a disco record
out now. It's very
interesting to hear
'Alexander's Ragtime Band'
disco."
```

"He's not joking," claims Tim. "I saw her sing it on TV. Very scary."

"Dahl's a revolutionary," states Scooter, truly believing it.

"Well," tries Bobby, "my mom says if you don't have anything nice to say then you shouldn't say anything at all."

"When're you gonna stop quoting your mom?" asks Scooter.

"What?" asks Bobby, incredulously. "There's an age limit?"

"Yeah," replies Reggie. "Seven."

"Sure, Reg." prods Scooter. "Like you don't do everything your mother says."

"Oh me? I have to," says Reggie rubbing his belly. "She's the only one who cooks for me and, *man*, can she cook."

"I'll second that." Tim hi-fives Reggie. "I love eating over at your house."

"Does she make that black food?" asks Scooter. "You know, grits and greens and all that?"

"First of all, it's not called black food," says Reggie. "It's Southern food. White people eat it too."

"You mean besides Tim?" jokes Scooter, just to wind him up.

"Fool." Reggie can't help but laugh with Scooter but leans over the seat to punch him in the arm just the same.

"Is everybody high but me?" Bobby wants to know.

"Dude." Scooter removes a joint from behind his ear. "We

wouldn't toke without you."

"Where's the rest of it?" asks Bobby.

"You were right," Tim tells him, removing the weed from his backpack. "Your sister shouldn't have to hold Woody's stash." He tosses the bag to Reggie.

"Not when we can do it for her," laughs Reggie, sticking his nose in the bag for a big whiff before passing it along to Scooter.

Scooter holds up the bag for Bobby to see, an idea forming in his teenage brain. "We can use the weed to get your bike back."

"Yeah," agrees Tim. "Like bait."

"You mean, barter," clarifies Bobby. "Bait would imply that we trick them in some way. I just want my bike back."

Scooter takes a bud, if you could call it that, from the bag. "In our neck of the woods this is Wisconsin ditch weed, but today, where we're going, this is goddamn Acapulco Gold."

Reggie slaps Scooter on the shoulder. "Now you're thinking."

"Shoot," says Bobby, squeezing the steering wheel. "I think we're lost."

"Chill, dude." Scooter gets a map from the glove compartment and unfolds it over his lap.

Bobby looks at Scooter. "My dad said to follow the lake until we get past Navy Pier."

Reggie checks out the back window to be sure. "We passed the pier a while ago," he says.

"And Grant Park," reports Tim.

"Soldier Field is just up ahead," announces Reggie, pointing over Bobby's shoulder.

"Now we just wait for 35th Street," says Scooter, his head buried in the map, "and go right ... until we hit Comiskey."

"We should've took the Dan Ryan Expressway," says Tim.

"You mean the Kennedy," suggests Reggie.

"No," says Tim. "I'm mean the Dan Ryan Expressway."

"You're right," says Scooter. "But you can drop the *expressway.* Just say the Dan Ryan."

"What?" asks Tim, getting annoyed. "I'm being graded on this?"

"Well," considers Scooter, "this is kind of a field trip."

"Guys," interrupts Bobby, looking out his window. "There's Soldier Field."

"Where Walter Payton plays football," adds an awestruck Tim.

"Sweetness," smiles Reggie, big and proud.

Tim smacks the roof. "Where Doug Plank lays guys out!"

But Bobby can't relax and enjoy the moment no matter how much he loves the Bears. Sure, the South Side is a trek and potentially hazardous to his health, but something else is nagging at the back of his mind. A bundle of nerves, he looks to Scooter for solace but his friend is lost in the weed, looking through it like he's going to find the meaning of life or at the very least a beef burrito. So Bobby drives on, not fully understanding what's got him so out of sorts. "This is crazy," he says, mostly to himself.

The boys have found 35th street and are heading west ... passing Michigan Avenue and then over the Dan Ryan, they eventually reach the Bridgeport neighborhood. Irish. Blue-collar. Working class. The heart of the South Side.

Eyes peeled, Bobby slowly drives the stationwagon past a group of rough looking white kids playing stickball in the street, like it's the 1950s. Real dead-end types, thinks Bobby. So, despite the heat, he quickly rolls up his window.

Scooter doesn't like much of what he sees either and looks over at Bobby, his laser blue eyes demanding the truth. "Are you sure this isn't about the girl?"

"I just want my bike back," snaps Bobby.

"Chill," Reggie tells him. "We get it, she was kind of a fox."

Bobby pulls over and parks the car along the curb. "Look, yes, Misty was, is, kind of a fox but--"

"Ahhh," smiles Reggie. "We have a name for her."

"*Fox on the run*," sings Tim, from the popular Sweet song.

"Guys, please don't say anything if we see her," requests Bobby. "And Tim, don't sing."

"It's the girl or the bike," Scooter tells him, taking in the foreign surroundings. "You can't have both."

"Yeah, how come I don't see any brothers?" asks Reggie, looking at all the kids. "Couldn't your old man just buy you a new bike?"

"He could, I suppose, but that's not always how life works," replies Bobby. "Besides, you can't replace a bike like that. It's like buying a puppy after your dog gets hit by a car. It doesn't solve the problem."

"Solved the problem for me," claims Tim, "after I got dumped by Stephanie."

"Sure," says Scooter. "That's because you replaced her with what's-his-name's sister."

"And she gave you a hand-job down on the rocks at NU," laughs Reggie.

The boys begin to hoot and howl when something smashes against the car, spoiling the fun.

"The fuck was that?" asks Bobby.

"That was the back window," answers Tim.

Scooter turns to him, concerned. "Did it crack?"

I don't think so," says Tim, looking it over. "Probably just a bird."

"Actually," points out Bobby, "that dude over there is giving us *the bird*."

The boys turn to see that one of the kids playing stickball, the batter no less, has stopped the game, choosing instead to extend his middle finger toward the stationwagon.

Tim climbs out the back before Bobby can even think to stop him and walks right over to the kid, ready to knock his lights out. "You got a problem?"

"Yeah." The South Sider, fourteen tops, doesn't back down, even though Tim's got fifty pounds on him. After all, he's still holding a Louisville Slugger. "Your stupid stationwagon just got in the way of me hitting a home run."

Tim looks at the bat the kid is holding and isn't impressed. "With that?"

"What?" asks the South Sider, all wise-guy like, "you don't like my bat?"

A couple of other kids walk up behind him, flanking him, but Tim isn't deterred. "Yeah, well, you won't like the bat either when I stick it up your ass."

Back in the stationwagon, Reggie stews as to how the next five minutes of his life is going to turn out and leads Scooter and Bobby out of the car to even up the numbers. Unfortunately, more kids come out from between the houses and revert the balance of power to the locals.

"Look," intervenes Bobby, "we don't want any trouble with you guys."

The South Sider puffs his scrawny chest out. "Didn't think so."

But Tim tells him how he really feels. "Fuck you."

Still, the South Sider doesn't back down. "Make me."

"Suck my dick."

"Whip it out."

"Guys," tries Bobby again. "This won't end well for any of us. Seriously, this is really just about my bike and obviously you don't have it so--"

"What kind of bike you talking about?" asks a smaller South Side kid, maybe twelve, dirt caked to his forehead. "A Chopper?"

"Similar, I guess, in style," replies Bobby, "but actually it's more of a bicycle."

"A bicycle?" laughs the smaller kid. "You lost your bicycle? Do you need a hug?"

The older South Sider pipes in again. "Fuck these homos."

"Hold it," says Scooter. "Are you calling us homos or are you hoping we're homos?"

"Ass-clown, said what?" caps the South Sider, not taking his chances with Scooter's question.

Bobby feels the need to assert himself. "Look, I can't be sure," he grants, "but I think maybe someone around here, not necessarily you guys, might have my bike."

"And what makes you think that?" asks the South Sider.

"Last night," Scooter tells him, "some dude from Bridgeport named Ian missed a boat home from Evanston."

"And," claims Bobby, "one minute my bike was there, the next..."

"Guy's got a girlfriend or something," adds Reggie. "Her name's Misty. She might live around here too."

"They're serious," laughs the younger kid. "What a bunch of cupcakes."

"You really came all the way from Evanston for a bicycle?" asks the South Sider.

"You don't understand," says Bobby. "It's a 5-speed Lemon Peeler. I've had it since I was nine. My Grampa gave it to me. My last Christmas present from him."

"Okay," says the South Sider. "Relax. I get it."

"If you could just put the word out about my bike," says Bobby. "And this Ian guy."

"Say we did," the South Sider wants to know, "what's in it for us?"

Scooter reaches for the joint tucked behind his ear and hands it to him. "More of this."

Chapter 4

RING MY BELL

In the basement of a brownstone, the younger of the two South Siders removes Led Zeppelin's *Physical Graffiti* from its cover and places the record on his Zenith turntable, part of a whole music console. For Joey, Zeppelin is an easy choice in 1979. However, outside of "Stairway to Heaven," Bobby would be the first to admit that Plant & Page were relatively unfamiliar to him, even though he essentially grew up on rock music. You see, before he began daydreaming about dancing at the Copacabana, he listened to the Beatles, the whole family did. And, of course, the Stones were everywhere. Plus, he knew just about every song on the Who's *Quadrophenia* thanks to Scooter.

Still, Zeppelin was off in its own corner. Ballsy guitars coupled with mystical lyrics only seemed to unnerve Bobby. And now, as if Bobby wasn't on edge enough, Joey lowers the needle on a particularly trippy selection, the fourth and final song of side three. At over six minutes, "Ten Years Gone" is just getting underway, something about eagles leaving the nest...

Meanwhile, his older brother Jack suggests a friendly game of pool, which just so happens to pit Evanston against Bridgeport; Bobby and Reggie facing off against brothers Jack and Joey. This is their place, their pool table, which is spent and visibly warped, though Reggie can't get enough of the giant cone of white chalk, like the kind you'd see at a bar.

Over in the corner, Scooter and Tim are sitting on a beat-up couch, rummaging through a stack of Marvel comic books dominated by the Hulk, who's been on a bit of a hot streak lately due to his hit TV show. As for the rest of the kids from the street ball game, they've agreed, per Jack's request, to scour the neighborhood for any info on Bobby's Stingray.

Joey finishes racking the balls, trying to act like the game doesn't mean much; either that or he's sure they're going to win. "Eight-ball. Call your pocket."

Jack hands Bobby a pool cue. "Guests break."

But before Bobby can do anything with it, Reggie walks over and takes the cue from him, full of confidence, even with an embarrassingly large amount of chalk on his hands. "Let me handle this." He places the cue ball in the appropriate spot and lines up his shot, stopping and starting a few times to loosen up and, of course, draw attention to himself.

In the meantime, as long as his bike is still in limbo, Bobby tries to make small-talk with Jack and stay on his good side. "Hey, you know, we've got a pool table too."

More interested in taking the edge off the heat, Jack plugs in a fan. "No shit?"

"Bumper pool actually," admits Bobby, "but it does the trick."

"I'm happy for you." Jack rolls his eyes as he reaches into a mini-fridge to retrieve a can of Schlitz. "Last one," he says, trying to act surprised. He tosses it to Bobby. "Loser goes down the corner for a 12-pack."

"Uh, sure." Bobby cracks it open, and though he doesn't particularly like the taste of beer, he's about to take an obligatory sip anyway when Reggie strikes the cue ball with all his might, inadvertently clearing the other balls, and the table, *straight into the can of beer*, which Bobby somehow manages to hold on to, much to everyone's surprise.

Shouts of appreciation and hi-fives in Bobby's honor ripple throughout the basement as they pass the dented can around for a drink, and though Bobby is flattered by the attention, he just looks at it as an opportunity to bond with the South Siders, anything to help find his bike and get out of there.

Bobby picks the cue ball up off the floor and hands it to Jack. "You got a cool set-up down here."

"I guess." Jack breaks, focused on winning the next round of beer, and sinks a solid.

"Nice," Bobby tells him.

Jack circles the table. "Four ball, in the corner." And sinks that too. "That's us," he announces. "We're solids."

"Are your parents home?" asks Bobby.

Joey hands the beer back to him. "I don't know," he replies, pretending to check. "Do you see any adults?"

"I meant upstairs," explains Bobby, taking a sip.

"This is the upstairs," Joey tells him. "Our parents are at work."

"Both of them?" asks Tim, as if this was a new concept to him.

"Yeah," replies Jack. "Our old man, on account of his knee, he don't get around like he used to so Ma does her part, you know, to help out."

"My mother volunteers at the high school," says Reggie. "In the office."

"That's fascinating," quips Jack. "Let's keep this game moving. And don't spill any beer on the table. Ted Kluszewski played on it the year we won the pennant."

"Who's we?" asks Reggie. "The Sox?"

Jack looks up from his shot. "Don't play stupid. 1959. Go-Go

Sox."

"After we clinched against the Indians," adds Joey, "our old man said the Fire Chief set the sirens off."

"I heard about that," says Tim. "Everyone panicked, thought it was an air-raid, the Russians or something."

"That's right," confirms Jack.

"When's the last time the Cubs did anything?" asks Joey, already knowing the answer.

"Came close in '69 but we gotta good team this year," insists Bobby. "Kingman's hitting balls out on Waveland, Reuschel's on his way to winning twenty games."

"Then the dog days'll come and the games'll start to matter," jumps in Joey, "and the Cubbies will choke."

Jack gives his little brother a simmer down look and hands the pool cue to Reggie. Then he walks over to where Tim and Scooter are sitting and pulls a huge glass bong out from behind the couch. "How 'bout we try some of your grass?"

"Right on." Scooter puts the struggles of Dr. Banner aside and pulls a bud out of the bag of weed. "How's this?"

"Fuckin' awesome," replies Jack. He turns up the stereo. "You boys ever listen to a little Zeppelin up in Evanston?"

> Through the eyes an' I sparkle,
> Senses growing keen
> Taste your love along the way,
> See your feathers preen
> Kind of makes me feel sometimes,
> Didn't have to grow
> We are eagles of one nest,
> The nest is in our soul
> --Led Zeppelin

"Or is it The Knack?" cracks Joey, scanning the table for his best shot. "*My my my my Sharona!*"

"I bet they disco in the suburbs," ribs Jack.

But Bobby's slow to catch on. "The, uh, Bee Gees are pretty tight."

"And The Who. We listen to a lot of Who." Scooter elbows Bobby. "You got your lighter?"

"No," Bobby remembers. "Woody has it."

"That's okay," says Joey, holding a blowtorch up to his shit-eating grin.

Scooter packs the bowl for Joey, who lights it for himself before passing it to him.

When Scooter's done he fills the bowl for Jack. "Here," he says, blowing a stream of smoke out of the side of his mouth...

Jack takes the bong from him. "You know about Disco Demolition Night?"

"Fuck yeah," replies Scooter, "Just bring a disco record to Comiskey next Thursday and you can get in for ninety-eight cents."

"It's Sox Park," corrects Joey. "No one calls it Comiskey."

"You guys going?" asks Reggie.

"Everybody's going," replies Jack, before taking a monstrous hit.

"What about *yous?*" asks Joey.

"This is a onetime trip coming down here," replies Bobby, still focused on his bike.

"What?" wonders Joey. "You got something against blowing up a bunch of disco records?"

"Of course not," says Scooter. "It's just that we'd have to watch a Sox game."

"Two games," Joey makes clear. "It's a twi-night

doubleheader."

"Exactly," maintains Reggie.

Jack finally exhales, smoke coming out of his nose like a dragon... "So why'd you come down here then?" he asks Bobby. "Why doesn't your rich Evanston daddy just buy you a new bike?"

"We asked him the same thing," says Reggie.

"Am I supposed to give up on it?" asks Bobby. "Just like that, after all these years?"

"Maybe you need a girlfriend," suggests Jack.

"He's got one," says Scooter. "Her name's Rosie."

Both sides of town laugh at Bobby until the bong finally makes its way over to him. "I've never done one of these before," he tells them.

"*One bong, three hits, and you're out,*" says Jack. "They make these puppies up in Milwaukee. The glass is hand blown."

"Hand blown?" wonders Tim. "That doesn't make any sense."

"You're thinking about girls," says Reggie. "You can't always make sense of the world thinking about girls."

Jack lights the bowl for Bobby. "Just breath in, long and slow."

Bobby does as he's told, taking a big hit, and manages to hold it in too, which impresses everyone until he violently coughs it back into the bong, *rocketing* the flaming bud across the room where it lands smack in the middle of the pool table...

"He snatched!" yells Joey, scrambling over to the table to flick the bud off the felt surface before it burns a hole through it.

"Sorry," coughs Bobby, still hacking away. "I need some fresh air." He hurries out the basement door into the alley where he's slow to adjust to the bright sunshine.

"I heard you were looking for me," comes a voice from somewhere within the white light.

Bobby grabs his nose with one hand while he reaches out with the other to break his fall...

Bobby slowly wakes up on a living room couch with a bag of frozen peas over one eye to find, "Misty?" He sits up confused. "What're you doing here?"

"I live here," she says, looking out the front window.

"This is your house?"

"It better be, otherwise we're both in trouble."

"Huh?"

"Yes," she smiles, walking over to him. "It's my house, or rather my dad's house, and I guess you met Ian."

"Not formally."

"Yeah, well, that's about as formal as my brother gets."

"So he isn't your boyfriend?"

"Do you want another black eye?"

"No, it's just that--"

"Don't get any stupid ideas," she tells him. "I don't do the boyfriend thing."

"The boyfriend thing?" Bobby tries to play it off. "I just came down here for my bicycle."

"Your bicycle," sighs Misty. "How manly of you." She heads to the kitchen. "You want something for your head?"

"Please."

"Something to wash it down with? 7UP, Coke?"

"7UP's cool."

She opens the refrigerator. "Is Sprite okay?"

"Sure," shrugs Bobby, noticing that she's wearing the Service Crew shorts.

"Guys are a waste of time," she says matter-of-factly. Then she reaches up high in a cupboard for a couple of glasses, causing her shirt to abandon her belly button.

Bobby tries not to stare at her exposed flesh but can't help himself. "Most of them, yeah."

Misty walks back into the living room, handing him a couple of aspirin and a glass of Sprite, and sits on the edge of the coffee table opposite him. "I take it you're the exception?"

"Oh, no. I'm definitely a waste of time," jokes Bobby, swallowing the tablets with one gulp from his drink.

"Keep talking," she says. "I promise I won't fall asleep."

Bobby's confused. Does she like him? Does he like her? Is she going to kill him? "Anyway, doesn't matter."

"Just so you know," she says, "I wasn't asking."

"Asking what?"

Misty takes back his drink even though he's not done and starts toward the kitchen again when she abruptly changes course, kissing an off-guard Bobby square on the lips.

Bobby reciprocates for a second or two but then backs off. "Whoa..."

"What's wrong?"

"Nothing, I just..." Bobby suspects his answer could mean the difference between another lip-lock or a headlock. "It's, I, uh, I've never had a girl make the first move before."

"Who said I made the first move?"

"I'm pretty sure you did," replies Bobby.

"You're full of shit."

"You say that like it's a bad thing," teases Bobby, pleased he's keeping up.

As is she. "So funny," she says, a smile forming on her beautiful freckled face. "This ain't the suburbs, you know. You could get hurt talkin' trash around here."

Bobby points to his eye. "I already did." He leans in and kisses her, his hand reaching for her hip...

But she brushes his hand away, kissing him back until Scooter barges in and ruins the occasion.

Scooter walks right up to Bobby. "Gimme some skin."

"What?" he asks, having almost forgotten. "You got my bike back? Who had it?"

"Who do you think?" says Scooter, nodding toward Misty. "It took some convincing, not to mention some of our pot."

Still, Bobby's stoked and slaps Scooter *five*. "Thanks, man."

"No problem," he says. "Reggie and Tim are tying it on top of the Mercury as we speak."

"Are we in a rush?" asks Bobby, winking at him.

However, Scooter isn't exactly catching on. "Mission accomplished, dude."

"No. Not really," says Bobby, following him outside to the street with Misty...

Where Reggie toots the horn, already behind the wheel with the Stingray secured to the roof. "I figured with you having one eye I should drive."

"Hold on," stalls Bobby. "Lemme check the bike's tied down properly." He looks over the ropes and knots but quickly finds himself drawn back to Misty. "Can I get your phone number?" he asks her.

"Come on, Bobby. I'm starving," complains Tim, hanging out the back window.

"We should so hit up White Castle on the way home," urges Scooter.

"You better go," says Misty.

"Wait." Bobby takes a moment to try and find something in the Mercury. He's got it. "Rocket to Russia," he smiles, handing over her neatly folded Ramones t-shirt as if it was a hallowed artifact. "My mom washed it."

Misty smiles, not necessarily sweet, thinks Bobby, but genuine, "Tell her, thank you."

"I'm glad your brother stole my bike," he says, getting into the car.

She leans in through the open window and kisses him on the cheek. "Me too," she whispers, handing him a crumpled piece of paper.

Reggie toots the horn again and they drive off, leaving Misty to wonder what just happened. Did she just fall for a boy from Evanston? Might as well be the moon. She tries to tell herself that it doesn't make any sense no matter how cute he is.

She sits on the steps of her house, a modest single-story brick bungalow, and sorts through her thoughts, when her dad walks up the sidewalk, looking drained after a shift at the firehouse.

"How's Mrs. McCuddy?" she asks, knowing her dad most likely stopped at the bar down the street.

"Ma was in great form tonight," confirms her dad. "She told us all stories of how Babe Ruth used to drink there when the Yankees were in town."

"Again?" she asks, with a knowing smile.

But her dad's serious. "Look, when all is said and done and you and me are long gone, McCuddy's will still be standing on the South Side of Chicago."

"I was just joking."

"Who was in the stationwagon?"

"Nobody."

"Is that why the bike Ian stole last night was on the roof?"

"They just came here to get it back," she says. "Doesn't have anything to do with me."

He looks at her, trying to read his teenage daughter. "He'll only break your heart."

"What?" She is so not talking about boys with her father. "Why do you always have to be so dramatic?"

"It's the only way you'll listen." He follows her into the house. "They always trade up on the North Shore. Bigger house.

Nicer car."

"Are you saying I'm not good enough?" asks Misty, getting irritated.

"No, not at all," he says, trying not to rile her up. "It's just that for some people, it's never good enough."

Chapter 5

PROVE IT ALL NIGHT

An overcast day on the boat ramp finds Bobby splayed out in a lawn chair behind a pair of Wayfarers. At his feet, a transistor radio is tuned into WLS, gently playing Supertramp's "The Logical Song." Bobby tries to sing along, *then they send me away*, but he's dozing off again.

Bobby can feel the wind kicking up across the lake. He knows he should take the flag down, to protect it. It's his job after all. His duty even. But he didn't get much sleep last night, not after what happened in Bridgeport with his bike--with Misty.

He just wants to turn off his brain for ten minutes. That's all it will take. Then he remembers Mr. Bradley cut short his morning sail, mentioning storms up in Wisconsin.

When the song ends, and the questions that run so deep still haven't been answered, Bobby gets up out of his chair and walks to the flag pole, where the breakwall meets the shore. He looks out over the water, scanning the sky, and sure enough dark clouds are brewing in Milwaukee.

So Bobby undoes the rope from its cleat and begins lowering the flag when someone jumps up in the Orca, scaring the crap out of him.

"Ahoy!" Scooter stands barefoot on the bow of an enormous

wooden rowboat, like one the Vikings might have used.

"Jesus, Scooter." Bobby takes a moment to collect his breath. "You about scared the crap outta me."

The Orca belongs to the city of Evanston. Unfortunately, no one knows what to do with it. At least, the adults don't.

Local teenagers have been known to secretly drag it off shore with the aid of a motorboat on a summer's night, then either anchoring the Orca or just letting it drift ... with a bunch of lifeguards and a few guys from the Service Crew aboard, plus some girls, of course, and a keg of beer.

But at the moment, the Orca sits on a trailer beside the boathouse at the top of the ramp--with just Scooter.

"How long have you been in there?" asks Bobby, before it dawns on him. "Did you spend the night in the Orca?"

"Dude, no offense, your couch is great and everything but it's pretty cool to sleep under the stars." Scooter points to the gray skies blanketing Evanston. "Even when you can't see them."

Bobby knows what he means, but he's worried about his friend. "Did you get baked?"

"No," replies Scooter, reaching back into the Orca for his sneakers. "I was afraid I'd get the munchies and starve to death."

"Ok, well, if you're not high and you still want something to eat, I brought a sack lunch. It's in the boathouse."

"Right on, I helped myself when you got here."

"You did?"

"Yeah, remind me to thank Barbara for the Snickers bar. That's a nice touch."

"The whole thing?" asks Bobby.

"You know," starts Scooter, on to something else. "She was digging you?"

"Who? Misty?"

Scooter laughs at the thought. "Like there's more than one girl that's in to you."

"What about Donna?" asks Bobby.

"Dude, as far as I know Donna's liked you ever since we saw *Enter The Dragon* at the Varsity. All the dudes from Nichols were hitting on her but she told everyone to take a hike, said she was with you."

Bobby tries to act like he doesn't think about it all the time. "Oh yeah, I remember that."

"And do you remember not doing shit about it?"

Bobby scratches his head. "I guess."

"So are you going to ignore Misty too?"

"I didn't ignore Donna," Bobby tells him. "I merely chose to pursue other options."

"Sure."

"I'm serious," says Bobby, lying his ass off. "I had my pick at Haven."

"Okay, whatever you say."

Bobby gets defensive. "Well if you're so concerned about my love life then why'd you run us out of Chicago yesterday?"

"We were in a war zone, dude."

"She kissed me," blurts out Bobby.

"Ok, now you sound like a girl."

"I kind of feel like a girl," says Bobby, not necessarily thrilled by the idea, "like I want to sing or something."

"How 'bout you stick to dancing?"

"Okay."

"Wasn't that her phone number Misty handed you last night?"

"Yeah, but what's the point?" asks Bobby. "It took us an hour to get down there yesterday and longer to get back."

"So what? Are you saying you wouldn't drive all the way to Hollywood to bang Farrah?"

"My dad prefers Cheryl Ladd."

"Well, yeah, I can see where he's coming from. I mean, Farrah's dating the Six Million Dollar Man. You don't really want to mess with that ... unless you're the Hulk."

"Right, the Hulk." Bobby folds the flag on his own this time. "Are you sure you're not high?"

"Just call Misty." Scooter gives Bobby a friendly shove. "What're you so afraid of?"

"I thought you said the South Side was a war zone."

"It is, ask her to come here."

"I guess I could. I mean, usually I'm grovelling at girls but Misty's just ... different. I can talk to her, like a guy almost, except she's really nice to look at."

"Does she have a friend?" asks Scooter.

"I'm supposed to be thinking of a threesome already?"

"No, a friend for me, idiot."

But before Bobby can respond, Woody walks out of the boathouse, salty as usual. "Don't you have any work to do, Bobby?"

"Sorry did we wake you," cracks Scooter, pulling a smushed pack of Camels out of his jeans pocket.

But Woody ignores him. "Bobby?"

"No boats," shrugs Bobby, "no work."

"The boathouse could use a cleaning," Woody tells him. "Toilets too."

"My job is the ramp," says Bobby, letting Woody know he's not a pushover. "The bathrooms are a Service Crew job."

"I don't know where those guys are," says Woody. "They're not picking up the radio."

"There was a big party at Lighthouse last night," butts in Scooter again, making a meal out of lighting a crumpled cigarette. "The fence got messed up. Gibbons, Combs, Lundberg, all those guys. They went up to fix it."

"He's right," confirms Bobby, covering for his co-workers. "I saw them load Big Bertha in the van."

"Wait," says Woody, putting his clipboard between his knees so he can go through his pockets. "Is that my lighter, Scooter?"

"Nah, dude." He holds it up, a blue one, almost tauntingly. "I got this off Bobby."

"Don't bullshit me," warns Woody. "I saw you come out of the boathouse earlier."

"I'm not," says Scooter, tossing the lighter to Bobby. "I gave it to him for his sixteenth birthday."

Woody doesn't know what to think, only that he's irritated. "Who's gonna clean the toilets then?"

"I'll start with the boathouse," tries Bobby, knowing full well his pals on the Service Crew were most likely napping somewhere. "If they're not back by the time I'm done, I'll get the heads."

"Fine." Woody starts to leave when he remembers the reason he came to see Bobby to begin with. "I heard you got your ass kicked yesterday."

"Not exactly my ass but--"

"Come on." Woody waves his finger at Bobby's sunglasses. "Let's see."

Bobby removes his Wayfarers to reveal a pretty good shiner. "Happy?"

Woody smiles and shakes his head. "You had to get your bike back, didn't you?"

"Why not?" asks Scooter. "Wouldn't you want to get something back that belongs to you?"

"When I want your opinion hippy boy," sneers Woody. "I'll beat it out of you."

"Anything else I can do for you?" asks Bobby, trying to snuff out Woody's fuse.

"Well, yeah," he replies, cautiously. "You ain't been messing around in your sister's room, have you?"

Bobby plays dumb. "Like what? Short-sheeting her bed?"

"No," shoots down Woody. "More like she's missing something."

"If you're talking about *Budokan*, that was Scooter," explains Bobby. "And Debbie said he could borrow it."

"I don't give a shit about Cheap *fucking* Trick," says Woody, his blood beginning to boil. "Do you have it or not?"

But Bobby holds his ground. "Have what?"

"If I find out you're dicking me over..." Woody bites his tongue in case Bobby's telling the truth.

Bobby isn't done though. "Did you really tell Debbie to go to Southern with you?"

Woody's less annoyed than baffled by Bobby's courage. "Say what?"

"She's got a scholarship to Cal," says Bobby, feeling the need to remind him. "Why in the world would you steer her to Carbondale?"

Woody grabs his crotch. "So I can get my rocks off."

Bobby makes a move for Woody, about to punch him, but Scooter slips in between them. "Dudes."

"That's what I thought," laughs Woody, heading back into the boathouse.

Bobby takes off one of his sneakers and *chucks* it at Woody, narrowly missing him as he goes inside.

"Don't worry," says Scooter. "He'll get his."

"He's such a ass-wipe."

"Agreed."

"Hey, thanks for getting my lighter back."

"No problem," says Scooter. "Now how 'bout calling Misty?"

Bobby smiles, proud of himself. "I already did." He nods down the shore to where Misty is walking up the beach...

With another girl. "She brought a friend?" asks Scooter. "For me?"

"Just behave yourself," Bobby tells him. "I think her name's Mary."

Scooter gets a load of Mary, who's rocking a rainbow tube top and green army pants. "Lookin' good," he smiles, wrapping his arm around his buddy's neck. "And to think they said it couldn't be done."

"What? About me?" asks Bobby. "About Misty? Who said that?"

Scooter pats him on the back. "Everyone."

When it really starts to pour, Woody lets Bobby off work. Not because he's a nice guy or anything. He just doesn't want Bobby collecting a paycheck sitting on his ass, even with the city of Evanston footing the bill. The way Woody figures it, his dad's a taxpayer, so that's just money that should trickle down to his own pocket.

Meanwhile, Bobby drives Scooter and the girls in his mom's Rabbit over to the Burger King on Clark Street to wait out the rain. And eat! Suddenly everyone's appetite is bigger than their wallet. Fortunately, Scooter is in a rather generous, more like horny, mood and digs deep into his pockets for a few singles and some change, paying for the whole lunch.

Bobby is ravenous, made more so now that his date with Misty is officially under way. But he doesn't know what to say to her after they order the food, surprising even himself when he nervously starts singing, "*Hold the pickles, hold the lettuce. Special orders don't upset us. All we ask is that you let us serve it your way...*"

The rather large lady behind the counter gives him a *zip it* look, but Bobby doesn't notice.

So Misty pokes him in the ribs. "You should probably stop

now," she tells him, thinking her date's really cute ... and possibly crazy.

As soon as the food comes Mary grabs a bag of fries off the tray, shoving a handful in her mouth. "Burger King's are so much better than Mickey D's."

"Lemme check." Scooter sticks a fry up each nostril, suspending them there by holding in his breath. Needless to say, Mary is duly impressed, and the two of them proceed to make small-talk, make fun of the other customers, and, when the rain stops, make out in the parking lot.

Back inside, Bobby and Misty are sipping on the last of their milkshakes as they dig a little deeper into each other's lives, trading stories like he and his friends used to trade baseball cards. Joking. Laughing. A little bit of gamesmanship.

And that's how they end up in the swimming pool that night without really planning on it, just breezing through the day on the buzz of being young and free--at least until curfew, not that any of them would admit they had any such time restrictions. Not at sixteen. After all, they weren't kids anymore--and anxious to prove it.

The girls don't seem to be weirded out that Bobby and Scooter have stripped down to their tighty-whities. And the boys certainly aren't complaining that Misty and Mary are in just their bras and panties, especially given that Mary's tube top is her bra, barely. This type of intimate, almost primal, coed get-together is a first for Bobby, and he's not sure how to react. He feels like pounding his chest and yelling to the skies, but knows he should just be cool and nod his head a lot.

It's early July and things are happening for Bobby this summer. He can sense a change. Priorities shifting. Desires lit. Hair growing under his armpits. Bobby looks over at Misty, trying to read her. She's beautiful and street-smart and interesting. And interesting to Bobby means different, someone who can teach him a trick or two.

He can't believe he didn't even know Misty two days ago. And now, in a backyard swimming pool in the heart of Wilmette, it's as if his every thought revolves around her. And she seems to like him too. At the moment though, she can't wrap her head around why Bobby keeps talking about disco.

"Dancing school?" Misty playfully splashes Bobby in the shallow end. "Really? Are you messing with me?"

"What else are they gonna call it?" asks Bobby, knowing Misty's asking *why* and not *what*. "You dance, it's a school." He splashes her back. "I went every Friday night, all of 8th grade."

"And they show you how to do the Hustle?" she asks.

"Yeah, all the latest dances," confirms Bobby. "This couple taught us, though I don't think they were a couple."

"Oh." Misty twists her long red hair, draining the excess water back into the pool.

"We're having a reunion tomorrow night," Bobby tells her, excited at just the thought.

"He just goes to meet girls," butts in Scooter, thinking he should cover for Bobby. "Don't let him fool you, there's some slow dancing going on too."

Bobby glares across the pool at Scooter, as if Misty is supposed to think he's never dated anyone. "The dancing," he says. "The dancing's the most important thing."

"Is he serious?" asks Mary, swimming over to them.

"Yeah," admits Scooter. "But, hey, don't look at me."

"What's wrong with dancing?" wonders Bobby.

"Nothing," Misty tells him. "Just seems like there's a lot of, I don't know, judging in disco."

"Like in the movie," says Mary. "Travolta was always competing when he danced."

"It's similar to figure skating at the Olympics," jokes Scooter.

"So disco has rules?" asks Misty.

"Life has rules," replies Bobby, getting defensive. "School, work, parents."

Misty smiles, captivating yet subtle. "There are no fucking rules in rock 'n' roll."

Mary climbs out of the pool. "At least not the rock we listen to on the South Side," she says, aware the boys are struggling not to stare at her fully developed, not to mention dripping, body.

Scooter can't believe his good luck. He would've made out with Mary whether she was hot or not. "Bobby doesn't get that disco's dead," he says, before cannonballing off the diving board.

"I take it you like the Village People," says Mary, holding up Bobby's t-shirt, a shot of the group on the *Cruisin'* cover.

"Of course," Bobby tells her. "I mean, 'Y.M.C.A.', how can that not get you going?"

"Going where?" jokes Misty. "Home?"

"Those guys never change their clothes," continues Mary, looking around for a towel that doesn't exist. "Cop. Indian Chief. Plumber. What's up with that?"

"They're probably just really into Halloween," replies Bobby, his sincerity singed by a sudden flame of doubt.

"I love Halloween," says Misty, going with it on Bobby's behalf.

"Oh yeah, I was into Halloween," starts Mary, slowly lowering her body back into the pool. "When I was a kid."

Bobby shakes his head, ignoring Mary, and instead focuses on Misty. "The Village People were on the cover of *Rolling Stone* in April," he informs her.

"I remember," she says. "My dad just about had a baby."

"The cover," Bobby goes on, unfazed by news of her dad's fit. "That basically means your legit."

"The Village People?" Mary splashes Bobby hard in the face. "Fuck off."

Misty looks over at Bobby, trying not to laugh. "Do you like get down to Donna Summer?"

But Bobby's still wiping the water out of his eyes. "I, uh, hold on."

Mary starts singing, "*Bad girls...*"

Misty chimes in, "*Talking about the sad girls.*"

Mary: "*Toot toot.*"

Misty: "*Hey, beep beep.*"

Scooter urges the two of them, fine as they are, to, "Keep it down."

"What do you mean, *keep it down*?" scoffs Mary.

"He means, we don't want to get busted," explains Bobby.

"Is it against the law to sing at night in the suburbs?" jokes Mary, thinking it may well be true.

"No," says Bobby, as a light switches on in the house across the lawn. He reaches for Misty's hand under water. "But it's not completely cool to sing at night in someone else's yard."

Misty's eyes go big. "So if you don't live here then who does?"

A patio door slides open, followed by shouting. It's a man. A really angry man, like he's done this a few too many times. "GET THE HELL OFF MY PROPERTY!"

"That dude," replies Scooter.

In mere seconds the four of them leap out the pool, scramble for their belongings, and hop over a six-foot wooden fence into the alley, just out of reach of a crusty old man in a bathrobe waving a rake over his head.

It isn't until then that Bobby realizes he's left behind, "My Village People t-shirt!"

"It's too late." Scooter quickly steers Bobby down the alley where they scatter into the darkness, hearts racing a million miles an hour, before reconvening at the Rabbit over on Greenwood.

Life as he likes it is unwinding rapidly and Bobby fumbles with the keys, dropping them at his feet.

"Bobby!" shouts Scooter, checking over his shoulder for the rake.

Mary runs up, panting. "What're we waiting for?"

Bobby finally unlocks the car and they pile in.

"Fire this thing up," orders Mary.

"Yeah, old dudes can be dangerous," says Scooter. "They've got nothing to lose."

Bobby starts the engine and jams the car into gear--

"Hold on," says Mary, straightening her top. "Where's Misty?"

"What?" Scooter turns around in his seat to discover that Misty isn't there. "Think she got caught?"

Mary rolls down the window and has a look, but it's too dark to see anything. "I thought she was ahead of me."

"I won't leave her," says Bobby, firmly.

"Gun it!" Misty runs up and dives through the window into the backseat. "He's right on my tail!"

Bobby peels out just as the old man catches up, waving the rake, cussing and hollering to nothing but the night, all the while unaware that what he really wants is to be fifty years younger and go with them.

Just to be safe, Bobby steers clear of the bigger roads and cuts through Wilmette's side streets, knowing it will get them back to Evanston around Dyche Stadium, where it's safe and quiet. On a typical Friday night in the neighborhood, Bobby's options are limited; basketball at Blomquist, a late movie at the Coronet, maybe a dance at the "Y," nothing new or of note. Not compared to having Misty in the car with him. He feels invigorated when he's with her. Wide awake. High on life. For Bobby, this girl is a whole new ballgame.

But he also feels somewhat like a fraud, as if he's fooled her into liking him. That he wouldn't have risked taking Misty pool hopping if he wasn't so desperate to impress her. But he did take her, he tells himself. He rose to the occasion. And, minus a very important t-shirt, came through relatively unscathed. However, now he has the burden of keeping it up.

Misty's in the back of the car with Mary, trying to catch her breath and explain what happened. Unfortunately, Bobby can't hear a word she's saying thanks to Scooter, who's cranking Tom Petty on the radio, clueless that he looks just like a teenage version of the rocker with his stringy blond hair.

Bobby has no idea if Misty's pissed or not, and he doesn't want to interrupt her so he just drives, anxious to get back to Evanston, out of trouble, wondering if he's supposed to give the girls a lift home. Beside him, Scooter turns the music up even louder, drumming along on the dashboard and waking up half of Wilmette. But it's fitting, Bobby thinks, since apparently Petty wasn't sure of what he had either.

I need to know
(I need to know)
I need to know
(I need to know)
If you think you're gonna leave
Then you better say so

--Tom Petty & The Heartbreakers

When the song is over Bobby turns down the radio and

pretends to find Misty in the rearview mirror, as if he hasn't been watching her the whole time. "What happened to you back there?"

Misty nonchalantly tosses him his Village People t-shirt. "Couldn't forget your boys."

Bobby can't believe it. "You. Went. Back?"

Misty sits up, leaning over the front seat. "Sorry I didn't have time to wash it like your mom," she teases.

"That's okay," he tells her, "That's wow. Right on. Thanks."

"The whole pool thing was totally bogus," bitches Mary.

"What?" asks Scooter, looking over his shoulder at the girls. "That was a blast."

Mary pulls up her tube top, giving Scooter less to drool over. "You could've told us that wasn't your house."

"Then you wouldn't have come," says Scooter.

Mary rolls her eyes. "Exactly."

"You had fun," Misty tells her. "Don't lie."

"Whatever. What's with these streets?" Mary sticks her head out the window. "They're all made of brick like Abraham Lincoln's still president or some bullshit."

"Wilmette has miles of roads like these," says Bobby, ignoring her nasty tone. "All the roads used to look like this."

"Feels like we should be in a horse and carriage," smiles Misty.

But Mary's not impressed. "I'm hungry."

"Mustard's is coming up," says Bobby. "What do you think?"

"It's probably closed," replies Scooter.

Mary looks at her friend. "We should go home."

But Misty nudges her. "Don't be such a buzzkill, Mary."

"I'm not," she says. "I'm tired."

"I thought it was hungry," Scooter reminds her.

"Hold on," Bobby tells them, not willing to let the evening end on a down note. "I know what we can do."

Back in Evanston, Tim follows a stone path in the dark, a pitcher of lemonade in one hand, a large bowl of fried chicken in the other. He smiles to himself as he reaches the garage, glad his friends have dropped in. You see, Tim doesn't mind the late night raid because he goes to a different high school than the rest of the boys, and he worries sometimes that they could drift apart. And, of course, they brought girls with them. That helps. A lot.

He uses his elbow to push up a light switch; revealing two snowmobiles, a wall of fishing rods, an old pair of wooden skis, one ski pole, sails to a sunfish, a drum kit, and a Fender guitar leaning inconspicuously against a Gibson amp. And, of course, his friends, still wet and reeking of chlorine.

"Pool hopping?" asks Tim, setting the chicken and lemonade down on a fold-up card table.

"Just one pool," replies Bobby.

"And not really a hop," clarifies Misty.

"More like a run for your life." Mary helps herself to the particularly meaty chicken leg that Scooter's eye-balling.

"Dang," says Scooter, making a show of it. "I guess I get the next two."

But Tim smacks him on the back of the head. "Girls first."

"Thanks," says Misty, picking up a piece. "If I don't feed Mary every couple of hours she turns into Linda Blair."

"No problem," smiles Tim, happy to please the girls so easily.

"Tim has three older brothers," explains Bobby. "I only ever see his mom in the kitchen making food. They eat, sleep, and play sports. That's it."

"They don't even have girlfriends," adds Tim.

"They must beat the shit out of you," laughs Mary, wandering over to the Fender. "Is someone in a band?"

"I am," says Scooter, casually.

"My family lets Scooter keep his equipment in here." Tim grabs a stack of plastic cups from a shelf for the lemonade. "He's got until the first snow, then my mom's gonna want to park her car in here."

Mary hands the guitar to Scooter, tempting him. "Do you play anything we know?"

"Might," replies Scooter, suddenly on the spot. He throws the guitar strap over his skinny shoulder. "I think I got one."

"You need help?" asks Tim, standing a milk crate on its end behind the drums.

"Sure." Scooter plugs his guitar into the amp and flicks on the switch, going through the jukebox in his head for a song that can light a fire under Mary. He knows it has to rock but wants to find something fitting for these two South Side girls. By the time he sets up the microphone stand, he's got it. "The one we did at the end of Gazzolo's party," he says, testing the mic.

"Gotcha," nods Tim. He puts a pillow on the crate and sits down. Then, once he's locked eyes with Scooter, he quickly counts out "one, two, three," and kicks the bass drum, launching Scooter into a fuzzed-up guitar riff, one dizzying chord after another of teenage rebellion by all-chick rock band The Runaways.

Scooter sings the first verse of "School Days," though not nearly as well as he plays guitar:

Used to be the trouble maker
Hated homework
Was a sweet heart-breaker
But now I have my dream
I'm so rowdy for eighteen

Bobby's eyes just about pop out of his head when Misty takes the mic from Scooter to sing lead vocals on the second verse:

Never read a single book
Hated homework and the dirty looks
Now I live my life
There's a lot I seen at eighteen

Scooter and Tim try their best to keep pace with Misty, who pretends to ride one of the snowmobiles while singing the chorus:

School Days, school days
I'm older now what will I find?
School day, school days
Starting to slip I'm losin' my mind

They're beginning to sound fairly decent when the power suddenly goes out, leaving them in the dark.

"What the fuck?" asks Mary, laughing nervously. "What happened?"

"My mom happened," replies Tim. "Must be after midnight." Tim pours everyone a lemonade. "A toast," he says, raising his cup into a ray of moonlight sneaking through the window.

"To what?" asks Mary.

"To eighteen," declares Bobby, hoping he nailed the right sentiment.

Scooter puts his guitar down and meets their cups in the middle. "Just two years to go."

"To The Runaways," says Mary.

"To freedom," adds Scooter.

Misty checks her watch. "Not if I don't get home soon."

Everyone quickly chugs their lemonade and files out the

garage door to the alley, except Tim, who, realizing he's the odd man out, saunters back inside his house.

Later, on the South Side of Chicago, Bobby and Misty sit on the front steps of her house, just hanging out, talking about nothing. Bridgeport is behaving itself at this time of night and the streets are pretty much empty, though Bobby is still wary of his surroundings. In fact, he's on a whole different frequency from the rest of his friends, picking up random shouting, slamming doors, even distant sirens that no one else seems to notice.

However, he's with Misty so he tries his best to play it cool. Plus, he wants to kiss her again, even if the parameters of their brief friendship haven't been set yet. The problem is that now Bobby's also running late as far as getting home, even for him, so he's saddled with the extra pressure of a ticking clock.

He wanted to kiss Misty at Burger King. But he didn't have his way. And he definitely wanted to kiss her at the pool. Of course, that idea got blown out of the water. Then the backup plan lost power at Tim's. And now he's behind enemy lines again.

Bobby curses to himself. What ever happened to the good old days when you could just call up a girl on the phone and ask her out? That's all you had to do. And the girl never knew if you were sweating it or not. The important thing was that you were a couple. And sometimes you barely knew her. Not that it mattered. It would be over in a couple of weeks, even days.

But Bobby feels like there's something more to Misty, something he can't quite wrap his head around. Some kind of beautiful mystery. The difference between looking at a rare treasure in a museum and discovering it for yourself at the bottom of the ocean.

"My sister saw Journey a couple of weeks ago at the Aragon Ballroom," Bobby tells her, trying to relate.

"My dad calls it the *Brawlroom*."

"That's funny, Debbie said there was a big fight after the show."

"It's true," says Misty. "Some hot ass bouncer quit his job on the spot, just so he could knock the shit outta some pricks."

"You were there?"

"My dad's a fireman," she explains. "I get to see all the shows for free."

"I've never been to a concert before," admits Bobby. "My parents won't let me. They think disco is just for adults."

"She's right. They're probably all doing rails."

"Rails?"

"Never mind."

"So firemen get free concert tickets for serving the community or something?"

"My dad's crew? No. But fire exits are more like fire entrances to him. Before Journey, he took me to see Van Halen in April. That was also at the Aragon. And Ted Nugent last Thanksgiving. AC/DC I've seen twice now. Once at the Riviera and last summer at Sox Park with Aerosmith for Summer Jam."

Bobby's impressed. "Those are some intense bands."

"He used to say, 'I can't leave you at home on your own so you might as well come with me'."

"That's cool of him."

"Yeah, but as you saw at the lake he can be a real asshole too, especially when he drinks."

"I just found out this summer that my dad goes to a bar."

Misty laughs. "All men go to bars, especially the married ones."

Bobby points to the Rabbit, "Look who's playing tonsil hockey in the backseat."

Misty shakes her head at the site of Scooter and Mary kissing in the car. "Get a room," she calls out.

"I didn't realize she liked him," says Bobby.

"Could've been anybody," shrugs Misty. "She just loves jamming her tongue down a guy's throat."

"I'll be sure to tell him that."

"No biggie. Scooter's not her type."

"What about you?" asks Bobby, feeling bold. "What's your type?"

"I don't have a type."

"Really?"

Misty sighs. "Took a bus and two trains just to get to Dempster Street."

"Are you saying I'm not worth it?"

"I asked my dad the same thing," admits Misty. "Besides, can't you find a girl closer to home? Maybe even someone with their own swimming pool?"

"What's that supposed to mean?"

"It means I like you and all. I just don't know where this whole you and me thing is going."

"Does it matter right now?" asks Bobby, trying to steady a sinking ship.

"Yes, it does."

"Well, does it matter that I can't stop thinking about you?"

She takes his hand. "Yeah, I guess that helps."

"Good," smiles Bobby, "'cause I was gonna say I can't stop thinking about you swimming in your underwear tonight but maybe that'd pushing it."

Misty elbows him in the ribs, nice and hard. "You think you're funny, don't you?"

Bobby knows he could come up with another line but goes in for a kiss instead...

When someone shouts, "Get the fuck off my girlfriend!"

Bobby and Misty look up to see Ian rip open the car door and drag Scooter into the street, punching and kicking him before he's had time to react. "You think you can come 'round my block and steal my girlfriend?" fumes Ian.

Bobby and Misty run out into the street. "Leave him alone," she begs her brother.

Bobby tries to pull Ian off Scooter but Jack and Joey appear out of nowhere to hold him back.

"This isn't your fight," Joey tells him.

"Ian, stop, we weren't doing anything," says Mary, as if it wasn't a big deal. "Nothing below the line."

"Ian, stop it!" screams Misty.

He considers it but only to taunt Scooter. "Fucker tried to give me some bad pot," lies Ian. "Some of that paraquat shit, thinks I don't know. And now he wants my girlfriend?"

"I'm not anybody's girlfriend," says Mary.

But while he's showing off, Scooter gets his bearings and, knowing the amount of shit he's in, grabs a rock from a pothole and *smashes* Ian's ear. Then before he can collect himself, Scooter delivers a mad flurry of punches, a few of which connect with Ian's face until Misty's brother is laid out on his back.

"That's enough," pleads Misty. "Please."

Scooter stops and Misty runs over to Ian, who's struggling to stand up. Meanwhile, Bobby shakes loose of Jack and Joey, the two of them quickly disappearing down the street. As for Mary, a fun night is ruined, and she decides to walk home.

"Let me help," says Bobby, thinking it would be a good idea to move Ian out of the street.

"No," says Misty, her lower lip trembling. "Please leave."

Bobby gets that it's not up for debate. "I'll, uh, call you."

Misty's eyes are beginning to tear. "Just... Go home."

Bobby and Scooter retreat to the Rabbit and drive off, leaving a distraught Misty to tend to her broken, bleeding brother.

Chapter 6

JUST WHAT I NEEDED

In 1978, 23-year-old Steve Dahl had a steady girlfriend and a Detroit radio gig when a station in the Windy City called, promising to double his salary if he would host a morning drive slot spinning rock 'n' roll records. Though flattered, Dahl, in part because of his girlfriend's family ties in Michigan, kindly declined. But when he asked his boss for a raise given that he was being courted, they told him to take a hike. So Dahl took his girl to Chicago and WDAI, where he created a show called "Rude Awakening."

Unfortunately, the ratings didn't take off as fast as executives anticipated and the station panicked, pulling a coup to change the musical format. Drastically. So get this, at midnight on New Year's Eve, the station went from playing "American Pie" to "Stayin' Alive". No joke. *Disco D.A.I.* was born. Dahl quit just in time to experience Chicago's *Blizzard of '79,* which was highlighted by close to seventeen inches of snow on Saturday January 13th and as far as Bobby and his friends were concerned, the "funnest" day ever. However, for an unemployed Dahl, it couldn't have been that thrilling. Then in February, to add insult to injury, Bob Denver hosted the Grammy Awards, dominated by, you guessed it, disco.

Things began to change in the spring of '79 when Dahl hooked up with another rock station in Chicago called *the Loop,* WLUP, and cool sidekick/newsman Garry Meier; the goal being to jump-start another morning show. As you can imagine, Dahl let his listeners know that he wasn't pleased with his former station for misleading him and uprooting the woman he hoped to marry.

And guess who took the brunt of the blame? Disco. And what Dahl referred to as *Disco D.I.E.* To make matters even more interesting, Dahl would drag the needle across a disco record on his show and blow it up--every day. Within weeks, this goofy act of defiance became a ritual for rock fans all over Chicagoland. Once Dahl blew up a disco record, "real good," listeners could enjoy the rest of their day with a smile and a sense of satisfaction.

That summer the distaste for disco was spreading like wildfire in Chicago, with Dahl and his infectious if not obnoxious personality as the focal point. Soon an anti-disco army was formed in his honor called the Insane Coho Lips, who came complete with their own song, the b-side to "Do You Think I'm Disco?" This rowdy pack of partiers, ranging in age from 13-33, turned Dahl's radio appearances at nightclubs like the Pointe East into rock 'n' roll rallies: "*Coho! Coho! Coho!*"

Back in Evanston, the boys are hanging out on the roof of Bobby's house, just relaxing outside his old 3rd floor bedroom, another hot summer day under the shadow of the elms with Dahl on the radio, rapping to Garry Meier:

```
"Steve, countdown to Disco
Demolition Night is on so why
don't you clarify for our
listeners once and for all why you
hate disco so much."
```

"Well, Garry, I hate disco because
you have to look perfect and your
hair has to be beautiful, and I
can't find a white three-piece
suit that fits me off the rack
that hangs well. And you gotta
have one of those."

"Okay, what else?" asks Garry.

"I'm allergic to gold jewelry."

"Go on."

"And I don't like piña coladas.
I'm allergic to coconuts. So what
does it hold for me?"

"Not much, I suppose."

"Plus, I can't dance," continues
Dahl. "One leg is shorter than the
other."

Tim laughs at Dahl and, getting a closer look at Bobby and
Scooter, keeps on laughing. "You two could be twins with those
black eyes."

Scooter turns away. "Dude, I'm done with the whole South
Side thing."

"What about Mary?" wonders Bobby, innocently enough.

But Scooter's not stupid. "More like, *what about Misty?*"

"I guess," mumbles Bobby.

Reggie climbs up on a tree branch hanging over the roof.
"You have to ask yourself if she's worth it, Bobby."

"I like her," he says softly, as if his subdued tone will win him sympathy points. "A lot."

"Bullshit." Tim punches Bobby in the thigh, trying to give him a charley horse.

"Hey..." Bobby rubs his sore leg but he's not denying it.

"You like that little ass of hers," says Tim.

"I never should've let her take the mic from me," grumbles Scooter.

"What do you mean?" asks Bobby.

Scooter looks over at his friend. "What do you mean what do you mean? She probably cast a spell on you with that Runaways song."

"That reminds me," says Bobby. "Did any of you guys find the Ramones record I asked for?" But his friends have nothing but blank looks on their faces. "Anyone?"

"The Ramones?" laughs Reggie. "Not at my house. I'm black. Remember? Black people don't do the Ramones. They scare the shit out of us."

Bobby looks to, "Scooter?"

"Nope," he frowns. "I won't contribute to the delinquency of a minor."

"Tim?" tries Bobby, eying his friend's backpack. "Is it in there? Is it? Come on."

Tim reaches into his backpack but digs around a little longer than necessary, teasing Bobby, before he pulls out an album. "This is their latest record." He hands it to Bobby. "Not their heaviest but totally rocks."

"Thanks." Bobby looks at the cartoon cover of the Ramones, all four in their usual tattered blue jeans, black leather jackets, white sneakers, and mops of dark hair.

"I'm gonna want that back," says Tim. "My cousin over in New England Village, that's his."

"Of course," agrees Bobby. "I know Tyler. Tell him thanks."

"Dude, she's trouble," warns Scooter. "Just listen to what the Ramones are singing about."

"Trouble is better than boring," contends Tim.

"Try telling that to my mother," says Reggie. "I'm lucky she even lets me out of the house sometimes."

Scooter lays back on the roof, hands behind his head, staring at the sky. "What's a disco boy like you gonna do with a rock n' roll girl anyway, Bobby?"

"Don't forget she's a Sox fan," says Reggie, climbing higher up the tree.

"I've had my run-ins with South Siders over the years," comes a man's voice.

The boys turn to see Bobby's dad, sticking his head out the window.

"They're a different breed," he says.

Scooter waves his fist in agreement. "Thank you."

"Leave well enough alone," continues his dad, joining them on the roof. "You got your bike back."

"I can't," claims Bobby. "Misty's just, I don't know, special."

"Slow special or hot special?" jokes Reggie.

"Hopefully both." Tim punches Bobby in the thigh again.

"Guys," appeals Bobby, trying to ignore the pain shooting through his leg. "She went back for my shirt."

"I'll give her that," allows Reggie.

"I'm telling you," says Bobby. "She's not like the girls around here."

"Different doesn't always mean better," says Scooter.

"He's right," seconds his Dad. "Did you know Donna's parents joined our country club?"

Bobby shrugs. "No."

"That means you can take tennis lessons with her. Maybe go

out for the team next year," says his dad. "She golfs too."

"Golf," repeats Reggie, climbing down the tree. "Tim, we gotta go caddie." Reggie lowers himself back onto the roof and steps through the window, saluting the boys, "Later."

Tim promptly follows him inside the house, reciting the caddie pledge. *"Show up, keep up, shut up."*

Once they're gone, Scooter turns to Bobby. "Donna digs you, dude." He pats his friend on the back, ready to put the case to rest. "And she lives on Sheridan Road."

"The east side," points out Bobby's dad. "You can swim from their place."

Bobby can't believe the sudden interest in his love life. "You two act like I'm getting married."

"No, but this girl you keep going on about lives clear across town. Two towns really," says his dad. "Do you remember how long I had to wait in line for gas last month?"

"I get it," Bobby tells them, still torn. "I don't know. I like Donna and she did just get her braces off--"

"I swear her tits have gotten bigger since school got out," blurts Scooter, before remembering his present company. "Sorry, Bobby's dad."

"That's okay," he tells him. "Tits are important."

"Dad," moans Bobby. "Relax."

Bobby's dad knows he's outlasted his welcome and goes back inside. "I'm just telling you the god's honest truth."

"Anyway," says Scooter, when they're alone. "Donna's the one who'll be at that dancing school reunion of yours."

"I know that but..."

"But what?" Scooter wants to know.

"But I called Misty this morning to see how her brother was."

"Not my favorite dude in the world," grants Scooter, "but I can't fault you for that. So?"

"So, yeah, well, in the process," says Bobby. "I think I kind of invited Misty to come tonight too."

Back in Bridgeport, Misty rummages through her bedroom closet while Mary relaxes on the bed, flipping through *Creem*, which bills itself as "America's Only Rock 'n' Roll Magazine."

"I think I have a crush on Ted Nugent," says Mary, staring at the cover of the Motor City Madman, a demonic snarl behind his Fu Manchu mustache.

Misty, though, has more pressing concerns. "I'm at a total loss here." She holds up one dress after another to her body without satisfaction before tossing them over her shoulder...

Where they pile up around Mary, who doesn't even notice. "It's as if Nugent has me in a stranglehold."

"Seriously, I need to find something to wear."

But Mary doesn't even look up. "I'm just trying to stay out of your way."

"Okay, okay." Misty digs deeper into her closet.

"Have you ever kissed someone with a mustache?" asks Mary, rolling over on the bed.

"Just your grandmother."

"That's not funny," laughs Mary. "She can't help it. I was so freaked out by her mustache as a kid I shaved it one time when she was sleeping."

"You did not."

"I did. I got half of it and then she started snoring so I had to stop."

"You are evil."

"What? I didn't want to cut her."

"How thoughtful of you."

Mary turns her attention back to the magazine. "I heard he lived in Palatine for a while."

"Who?"

"*Nugent.*"

"Are you even listening to me?" asks Misty. "I need help."

"Fine, but in case you were wondering, I'm not goin' to dancing school."

"Well I'm not goin' either if I can't find the right dress."

"What is it with you?" wonders Mary. "He beat up your brother."

"That was Scooter. The guy who had his hand down your pants. Remember?"

"I was wearing underwear."

"Anyway," sighs Misty. "This has nothing to do with Scooter."

"Okay, I get it. Bobby's tall and not bad to look at. I'll give you that but most guys from the suburbs are a bunch of mama's boys."

"Contrary to popular belief, Mary, nice isn't a bad thing. And who says I want to live in the city the rest of my life?"

"What's so bad about the city?"

"Nothing. It's just that they're other places, other things."

"Other people?"

"Yes, besides I just feel good when I'm with Bobby."

"You're such a fucking princess."

"It doesn't matter," gripes Misty. "I don't have a dress."

"Who says you need a dress to disco?"

"What do you mean?"

Mary tosses aside the magazine and gets up off the bed. "We should perm your hair."

"Do we have time?"

"Probably not." Mary sits Misty down on a chair in front of the mirror above her nightstand. "Let's start with your eye shadow. What color says *boogie oogie oogie* to you?"

Later that night, outside the Woman's Club of Evanston, Bobby reaches into his back pocket for a comb and runs it through his hair for the zillionth time, even if it hasn't moved a fraction of an inch since he left home. He's nervous, wondering if Misty is going to show up or if maybe Donna has been the right move all along.

He's borrowed the leisure suit again, which means he had to listen to his dad's never-ending knowledge of the female species before he left home. This time, his dad punctuated his point for Donna with the first commandment of real estate; *location, location, location*. And, as usual, his dad made a lot of sense. Of course, Bobby would never admit that to him.

Reggie joins Bobby at the doors to the Woman's Club, looking equally funky in a double-breasted jean jacket and matching bell-bottoms, embroidered with flowers. "We should get in there," he says, as 8th grade boys and girls in suits and ties and dresses and heels wade past them into the building.

But Bobby's not in a hurry. "We got time."

"I don't think she's coming, man."

"Who?"

"Now who's jive talkin'?"

"Okay, but she could still show up."

"Misty doesn't even drive," points out Reggie. "And you can't expect her to keep taking the 'L' down here, especially at night."

"I know," shrugs Bobby. "You're right."

"Besides, Donna will be here with Patti which means we can all hang out later."

"I thought your mom made you break up with Patti?"

"She did, but we still fool around sometimes."

"Really?"

"Yeah, man."

Bobby wonders if he'll ever be able to understand girls. "You bring anything to drink?"

"For sure." Reggie checks to see that no one is watching and removes a pint of Southern Comfort from the inside of his jacket. He hands it to Bobby. "Be cool."

Bobby takes a quick discreet drink and gives the bottle back to Reggie. "Thanks. That's..." He shivers. "Damn."

Reggie laughs at him. "There's nothing like a little southern hospitality, huh?"

"I guess so," replies Bobby, not used to the taste of hard alcohol.

"I'll have some of that," says a girl's voice coming up from behind them.

The boys turn to see Patti skating over, ready to dance the night away in a bright yellow mini-dress and matching headband.

"Here." Reggie hands her the bottle, sharing a knowing smile.

Donna catches up to them, dressed a little more conservatively in pumps and a blue silk dress, pinched at the waist with an over-sized black leather belt. "Hi," she says, letting her incredible green eyes do the rest of the talking for her.

Not that Bobby can figure her out. You see, Donna always has some kind of force field up as far as he can tell. And, truth be told, it unnerves him. Like if he dug past the pretty face and entrancing eyes he might accidentally rupture a power line. And then he'd have to fix it, putting him under her spell for life.

"How's it goin?" he asks Donna, unsure if she knows what's gone down the last couple days on the South Side.

"Cubs won today," she replies, sweetly. "Kenny Hotlzman pitched the whole game."

"He did," says Bobby. "It was impressive."

"Would you two shut up about the Cubs?" asks Patti, pouring a steady stream of whiskey into her can of Tab. "How'd you guys get the booze?"

"Had it delivered," grins Reggie.

"Taxi?" she asks.

Reggie nods. "You'd think they would've caught on by now."

"That's what Evanston gets for not having a stupid liquor store." Patti screws the cap back on and holds the bottle out to Reggie, but Bobby intercepts it.

"I think I need a little more," he says, taking another drink.

"No problem." Reggie pats Bobby on the shoulder. "I got you covered."

"It's so weird being here again," says Patti. "I can't tell if 8th grade seems like a long time ago or just yesterday."

"It was two years ago if you need any help," jokes Reggie.

Patti pinches Reggie's arm. "Don't be a dick."

"I don't know if I can remember all the steps," worries Donna.

"It'll come back to you," Bobby assures her, "once you get out on the dance floor."

"*Do a little dance, make a little love,*" sings Patti, "*get down tonight.*"

"Chill out," groans Donna, sneaking a look at Bobby's reaction.

But Bobby's not giving anything away. "Remember," he tells them. "We're supposed to be chaperones tonight."

"How'd I get talked into this?" asks Patti.

"Free liquor," replies Reggie, winking at her.

"How much time do we have?" wonders Donna.

Bobby checks his watch. "Not enough." Then he looks to Patti. "Are you gonna take those roller skates off?"

Patti frowns. "What do you think?"

But Bobby doesn't know what to think anymore as he leads the four of them inside the building, taking one last glance over his shoulder for Misty...

The Woman's Club of Evanston has been a beacon of community service on the North Shore since 1889. And tonight, the clubhouse has been cleared to teach local teenagers how to dance properly; promising that if they try to learn a Waltz or a Foxtrot, they'll teach them *modern* dance.

On one side of the ballroom floor, Bobby and Reggie stand with a group of twenty or so boys while Donna and Patti wait with an equal amount of girls, maybe a little more, on the other. In the center of the room are the two dance instructors, somewhere in their forties, guesses Bobby, the same pair who taught the class when a bunch of them from Haven went.

The instructors, dressed in formal evening attire, go over some new moves, demonstrating a box-step to a slow dance again and again for the kids, some of whom are eager to make contact with the opposite sex, whereas others are ready to run for their lives.

"Think he's doing her?" asks Reggie, watching the man pull the woman close to him with a bit of pizazz.

"I think he's just into the dancing," replies Bobby, one eye on the entrance to the ballroom.

"Maybe a bit too much, if you catch my drift."

"Not really," says Bobby.

"Okay but her husband can't be too pleased about it."

"If he was alive."

"He kicked it?"

"Slipped on the ice last Christmas coming out of the Jewel."

"That's the guy?" asks Reggie, "Wasn't it Dominick's though?"

"Could've been."

"So she's probably all into his happy hands, whatever his intentions."

"I guess you gotta take what you can get."

"What about you?" asks Reggie.

"Me?" replies Bobby, as if it wasn't obvious enough. "Where's that bottle?"

"Here." Reggie gives him the Southern Comfort again.

"Thanks." Bobby takes a swig, watching Donna across the room, where she spots him, not by accident, and gives him a hopeful little wave.

"You see that?" asks Reggie. "That's your opening, my man."

Bobby takes another, bigger drink. "Better late than never, right?"

Misty's dad stands out in the hallway, tapping a bottle of Budweiser against his daughter's bedroom door.

"Can I come in?" he asks.

Mary opens the door, just a crack. "She's getting dressed," she tells him, a teen cocktail of indifference and attitude.

He grunts. "I just want to know what happened to Ian."

"The usual," says Mary. "He started a fight he couldn't finish."

"With one of those Evanston boys?"

"Uh-huh."

"So I take it that's the end of Misty and," taking a celebratory drink of his beer, "what's his name?"

Misty speaks up from behind the door. "Nope."

"What do you mean, *nope*?" he asks. "Your brother's a mess."

"Bobby had nothing to do with it," Misty tells him.

"Are you gonna let me in or not?" he wants to know, trying to tame his temper.

Mary opens the door to reveal Misty, looking electric in black leather hot pants and matching go-go boots, with big hoop earrings and tons of sparkly blue eyeshadow. And she's got on this red stretch sequin bandeau top, which matches the color of her flipped and feathered hair but doesn't cover her midriff. At all. Her dad is speechless.

"In fact," Misty announces, sorting out her silver mini-purse. "I'm taking the 'L' up to Evanston right now to see him."

But her dad isn't on board with that plan. "Your mother would never let you outta the house dressed like that."

"We'll never know," says Misty, breezing by him. "Besides, most of this was hers."

"You're sixteen," he says, trailing her down the stairs.

"Not for long."

"Sorry," he tells her, about to lose his shit. "You're not getting on the train in that outfit."

Tonight, however, Misty's defiant. "You can't stop me."

But her dad hustles around her and blocks the front door. "I just did."

Toward the end of class the instructors take a breather, allowing Bobby to lead the 8th graders in a dance. So everyone waits while he flips through the available vinyl for just the right song. And there it is. Already one of the biggest albums of the year. Peaches with the beads in her hair. Herb with the cool necklace. Both of them staring tenderly into each other's eyes.

If Donna's hoping for "Reunited" and a chance to snuggle Bobby though, she'll have to wait. You see, Bobby's determined to pump some life into the class, opting for the song just before it on side one, "Shake Your Groove Thing."

However, contrary to the song's title, this isn't going to be a freestyle dance either. Instead, Bobby organizes the kids in lines; some just girls, some boys, the one in back a mix of whoever's left.

Then Bobby demonstrates a couple of basic steps and has the kids try to mimic him, in unison. Unfortunately, it doesn't go as planned so, ready or not, he puts the song on.

Bobby dances along with them, working his way up and down

the rows, while Reggie (up front) and Donna (in back) try to lead by example.

As for Patti, she just skates in circles around the floor, occasionally throwing in a heel-toe or a crossover turn to distract the 8th grade boys.

Bobby is totally getting into the music. The dance floor is his second home, where he can relax and cut loose. He's coaching the kids, encouraging them, when he comes upon Donna, doing her best to guide the group in the last row. He's impressed. And relieved. As if the choice between the two girls has been made for him.

Groovin' loose or heart to heart
We put in motion every single part
Funky sounds wall to wall
We're bumpin' booties, havin' us a ball, ya'll

--Peaches & Herb

Bobby dances closer to Donna... "You're doing a great job."

"Thanks," she tells him, over the music. "It's coming back to me. Sort of."

"Maybe we could practice together some time?"

"Yeah," she smiles, her heart skipping a beat. "I'd like that."

Misty's dad pulls his orange Dodge Dart over to the curb, parking in front of the Woman's Club of Evanston. But he leaves the engine running, fully prepared to take off again should his daughter so much as blink.

He looks her over one last time, still in the clothes he never approved of, and shakes his head. "Are you sure you wanna do this?" he asks her.

"The whole disco thing seems a bit weird but Bobby... I'm hoping he's worth it."

"You know," he says, lighting a Marlboro, "they're a lot of snobs on the North Shore-"

"I get it, dad."

"Yeah, but they're different up here. They'll say you don't belong."

"Maybe I don't. And maybe," she says, checking her hair in the rearview mirror, "I don't care."

"And maybe they just don't know you like I do."

"I love you, dad."

He leans over and kisses her on the forehead. "I'll wait for you. It's not a problem."

"No... Thanks." She gets out of the car. "I'll take it from here."

"Good luck, baby." He waits for her to close the door and then reaches for a Filbert's root beer in the cooler he keeps behind his seat, holding the bottle to his overheated forehead as he fishes in the glove compartment for the right 8-track.

He puts in a favorite of his, Foghat's *Fool for the city*, and opens the root beer, praying everything works out for Misty, who's wobbling up the steps to the Woman's Club in the same go-go boots that once belonged to his wife.

Under the dimmed lights of the ballroom, 8th graders slow dance to Heatwave's mellow jam "Always and Forever," while the two instructors make sure the kids behave in such close proximity to the opposite sex. And, except for a couple of pinched butts, an elbow grazing a boob, and an inadvertent boner, most everyone is conducting themselves properly.

Misty steps inside the front door, feeling good, looking great, trying to ignore the butterflies hatching in her stomach as she searches for Bobby out on the dance floor.

However, Misty's not having any luck because Bobby is on the other side of the ballroom, still leading the class. He walks over to a microphone and turns it on, waiting for the right moment to get a word in while the song continues:

There'll always be sunshine
When I look at you
It's something I can't explain
Just the things that you do

--Heatwave

Bobby finds a break in the vocal and speaks into the mic. "All right, boys and girls, you know what to do." Then he lowers his voice to a whisper, "*Snowball...*"

In dancing lingo, *snowball* means that Bobby wants the kids to change partners. That way, since the girls outnumber the boys, everyone gets a chance to dance. As for himself, he's just about given up the idea of Misty ever showing up and figures this is as good a time as any to seal the deal with Donna. But he can't find her.

Reggie tugs on Bobby's arm. "She's waiting for you, man." He points Donna out, over in the corner, fending off a pack of boys offering nothing more than perspiration and pimples.

"You think so?"

"Yeah, man, quit being a wuss."

"Me?" Bobby pushes up the sleeves of his jacket, a nervous wreck. "I got this," he feigns. Eyes glossed over, he walks across the floor, unaware that Misty is waving to him in the doorway.

He squeezes past the growing congregation of 8th grade boys and stops in front of Donna, holding out his hand, which is practically shaking. "Should we give it a go?"

"Definitely." Donna takes his hand in hers, grateful to be rescued by the love of her young life. And, it's true. She's never really dated anyone, opting instead to let Patti get the word out every couple of years that she still likes Bobby.

He places his free hand on her hip, and they begin to dance to the song... "It's been a fun night," tries Bobby.

"We're just getting started, aren't we?"

"Right."

"Patti's parents drove up to Lake Geneva." Donna pulls him close, her warm breath tickling the inside of his ear. "The house is empty."

Bobby's mind races to a dark bedroom at Patti's. He wonders what Donna expects of him, especially if Reggie and Patti disappear for a while. Could this be it? His first time? He wants that, at least for bragging rights amongst his friends. He's not sure if Reggie brought any condoms though. And then he remembers, "Patti's dad asked me to cut their lawn while they're away."

Donna laughs at Bobby, at his innocence. He makes her feel comfortable. "You smell good," she tells him.

"It's, uh, Old Spice."

Donna rubs the back of her hand across his barren cheek. "I didn't know you shaved."

"I don't," he explains. "Just getting ready."

"Oh, Bobby," coos Donna, resting her head on his shoulder.

The dancing part Bobby can handle, but he knows the rest of his game needs work. He slowly rocks Donna back and forth. Sure, he likes her. And she's super-hot. Yet, something just doesn't feel right when he's with her. Like he can't relax, even though he wants to badly.

Meanwhile, Misty is on to them, marching across the dance floor toward Bobby and Donna with a bone to pick...

But Donna spots her first, quickly catching on that this redhead must be the city girl that Patti's been warning her about. So, seizing the moment, Donna takes matters into her own hands, distracting Bobby with a long wet kiss, which, to his relief, he has no trouble giving in to.

Misty, understandably, is furious. "Bobby!"

Bobby unlocks tongues and turns to see Misty, parting a final sea of dancers to reach him in an out of this world disco outfit, which distracts him, in a good way, kind of. "Hey, I, um, damn, I didn't think you were coming."

The kids around them stop dancing, curious to see what's up with the bitter redhead.

"You invited me," attests Misty, her hand forming into a fist. "Didn't you?"

Bobby knows she's right. "Uh, yeah, I, uh..."

Misty starts to speak again but is rudely interrupted by an 8th grade boy, one of the O'Hollearn brothers no less. "Nice outfit," he calls out.

"For a hooker," adds his dance partner, surely more jealous than offended.

Laughter erupts from the kids as one of the instructors stops the song abruptly to find out what's causing all the commotion.

Frustrated, Misty starts for the door... But not before breaking the heel on one of her go-go boots, causing her to stumble and almost fall over. Completely humiliated, she kicks the boot off, leaving it behind as she rushes out of the ballroom ready to strangle the nearest tree.

Bobby starts after her but Reggie stops him: "Leave her, man. It's over."

Bobby picks up the boot anyway and just stares at it for a

moment before coming to a conclusion. "No, it's not."

Donna's heart drops to her stomach. "Bobby?"

"Sorry, Donna." Bobby races outside to the street where he spots Misty just as she ducks inside the Dart.

"What happened?" her dad wants to know, one eye on Bobby racing toward them.

"I told you not to wait," she replies, black tears of mascara streaming down her cheeks.

He looks at her feet, confused. "But you're missing a boot."

"Can we just go home?" she cries.

"Misty!" Bobby reaches the car, waving the boot. "Wait!"

"Oh, I got ya." With Foghat's "Slow Drive" on the stereo, her dad puts the car in gear and takes off...

But Bobby jumps face first onto the hood of the Dart and, seeing as Misty's dad keeps driving, regrets it immediately. Holding on for his life, and with one hand still clinging to her boot, Bobby pleads with her through the windshield. "Misty, I'm sorry! I didn't think you were coming! I thought you blew me off!"

She does her best to ignore him while her dad drives through downtown Evanston, past the Orrington Hotel and the library, then left on Church street by the Carlson Building toward the lake, not too fast, but slowing down and speeding up to try and shake Bobby off the car, the last time Bobby smacking his forehead into the windshield.

"Get off of the car!" she implores him.

But Bobby holds on even tighter. "Not until you agree to talk to me."

Misty is sure he's going to get hurt and turns to her dad, "Keep driving."

Bobby won't give up though. "You're the one that I want, Misty!"

She shakes her head. "That's Travolta talking."

"It's a good line," insists Bobby.

"I believe Travolta *sang* it," butts in her dad. "And in case you're curious, boy, I still don't like you."

Part of Misty is turned on by Bobby's bravery, even if it's a waste. She looks over at her dad. "I wanna go home."

Her dad smiles, a crooked tooth catching the light off a streetlamp, and slams his foot on the gas, making a tire screeching turn on Hinman Avenue toward the city.

Still, Bobby holds on, with just the one hand, by his fingertips. But when the car straightens out, Bobby rolls off the hood...

Slightly disorientated, his ego more bruised than his body, Bobby sits in the middle of the street clutching Misty's go-go boot like a long-lost teddy bear as the South Side girl once again fades into a hot summer's night.

Chapter 7

HEART OF GLASS

In 1927, Bill Veeck was a teenager selling popcorn at Wrigley Field when he suggested the Cubs grow ivy on the outfield wall, and a few years later he helped plant it. When World War II broke out, he volunteered to fight and became a Marine, losing a leg in the battle for the South Pacific. After the war, Veeck bought the Cleveland Indians and signed Larry Doby, the first black man to play in the American League. And in 1960, as owner of the Chicago White Sox, he installed baseball's first exploding scoreboard at Comiskey Park, setting off fireworks after every Sox player hit a home run. Oh, and as for the wooden leg he got, Veeck, a cigarette smoker, carved an ashtray into it.

Obviously, all of these acts are memorable if not totally cool and gained Veeck a reputation as someone who wasn't afraid to get a little creative, especially when it came to filling seats at a baseball game. Case in point, the August afternoon in 1951 when he called on Eddie Gaedel, a fellow Chicagoan and war vet, to pinch-hit against the Tigers. At 3 feet, 7 inches, Gaedel instantly became the shortest player in baseball history, walking in his only plate appearance on four straight pitches. The number on the back of his jersey, *1/8*.

Fast forward to 1979, when Veeck, in his second stint as owner of the White Sox, wanted to see if his son Mike had a feel

100

for the family business. To that end, he gave the 28-year-old control of a team promotion at a time when the club was in desperate need of a hit. Just two years after sluggers Oscar Gamble, Richie Zisk and the rest of the South Side Hitmen brought some real excitement to Comiskey, the White Sox were playing lousy and struggling at the box office.

Mike knew to be a Veeck was to think outside the box, so he did, back to his days in a rock band. With disco reaching a fever pitch on the national music charts, Mike wanted to find a way to pay homage to his rock 'n' roll roots at the ballpark. How that would play out as a promotion, however, he wasn't exactly sure.

Eventually he talked to Jeff Schwartz, a rock aficionado who was the general sales manager at the Loop. Schwartz told Mike to give a listen to Dahl in the morning, the idea being to capitalize on the fervor surrounding Dahl and the Insane Coho Lips.

So Mike tuned in, and was turned on, taking special delight each day when Dahl blew up a disco record. Pretty soon plans to demolish a whole box of disco records between games of a doubleheader was given a formal name, Disco Demolition Night. And a date, July 12th. Before he knew it, Mike Veeck's big chance to get some people out to Comiskey Park and impress his dad was just days away.

Bobby doesn't exactly plan on jumping up and down like a lunatic the morning after the debacle at dancing school. It's more a feeling inside of him that gets his feet moving, an emotion that he can't put into words but has to come out.

Usually in the summer, if he's not working on the lakefront, Bobby sleeps in. However, he's up with the sun today, his mind locked in on Misty, trying to formulate a game plan to win her back.

But despite playing out several different scenarios in which he goes to Bridgeport with chocolates or flowers or both, he can't think of anything that doesn't make him look like a complete tool.

So, seeking a little sisterly advice, Bobby walks up the stairs to the kitchen, right past his dad who's cooking sausages on the stove, and up to Debbie's room.

Unfortunately, Debbie isn't around. But Bobby doesn't leave. In fact, he realizes it wasn't Debbie that he wanted. He just stands there in the middle of her room, frozen, deep in thought, allowing whatever's bubbling in his brain to rise to the surface.

When it hits him, Bobby shoots like a bolt of lightning down to the kitchen, past his confused dad, who's now burning the sausages, all the way to the basement, where he grabs the record Tim brought over and heads straight back up to Debbie's room.

The Ramones, Bobby hopes, can be his conduit to Misty, the key to getting her back. Putting on his sister's headphones, he lowers the needle to the first song on *Road To Ruin* and begins to slowly jump up and down. He can't help it:

Hanging out on Second Avenue
Eating chicken vindaloo
I just want to be with you
I just want to have something to do

--The Ramones

Bobby's dad can't figure out for the life of him how his growing teenage boy keeps passing through the kitchen without wolfing down a sausage or seven. He scratches his thinning head of hair, gently so that nothing falls out. Maybe he really does overcook them, he thinks. He thought everyone was just teasing him when he grilled on the 4th.

Bobby's dad marches upstairs and down the hall, determined

to get the straight scoop on his sausages, when he finds Bobby bouncing off the walls in Debbie's room.

But Bobby's oblivious and doesn't even see him in the doorway. He just keeps on *jumping* and *kicking* and *punching* to the punk rock beat, three steady notes in under three minutes.

His dad watches him, wondering what combination of drugs his boy could be on. He's never seen Bobby in such a spastic state. And his normally immaculate hair is in chaos, not to mention the black eye. Frankly, he's concerned. He can hear anarchy coming straight through the headphones.

Bobby's dad can't take it anymore and walks over to the turntable. He doesn't bother with the needle though. He just unplugs it from the wall, the record spinning slower and slower...

Until Bobby finally notices Joey Ramone's wail turning into a whimper and looks up to see his dad. He stops dancing and puts the headphones around his neck, catching his breath, as if nothing unusual is going on. "What's up?"

"What's up?" his dad repeats. "Well, for starters, what on god's green earth is that noise you're listening to?"

"It's the Ramones, dad."

"The who?"

"No, not The Who, the Ramones."

"Don't be a smart-alack.

"I'm not. It's just--"

"What? You came home a mess last night at who knows what hour and now you're blaring this crazy suicide music like you're about to have a seizure."

"It's just a song."

"If you want to give rock a try why don't you start with something easy, like Kansas or Seals and Crofts."

"It's not that." Bobby plops down on the bean bag, ready to spill. "I kissed Donna at dancing school last night."

"It's about time," says his dad, rubbing his hands together excitedly.

"In front of Misty, the South Side girl."

"Oh no."

"And she's pissed."

"Oh god."

"Then one of the O'Hollearns said something stupid."

"I bet I know which one."

"So Misty runs off but her boot breaks and she almost falls over in front of like everyone."

"Oh shit."

"And then there was a car ... mix-up with her dad--"

"A car mix-up?" his dad wants to know.

"Never mind, the point is, she's probably never speaking to me again."

"Can you blame her?" His dad picks up the Ramones album. "What are they, brothers?"

"Not really. Not by blood at least."

"Whatever happened to my disco dancing son?" needles his dad. "I kinda miss him."

"Dad... I'm surprised as anyone to be saying this, but I think that song just made me feel better."

"About what?"

"I don't know," replies Bobby, giving it thought. "Everything."

His dad smiles. "Well, I'll be dammed."

"What?"

"She's got you."

"Got me?"

"You're hooked," laughs his dad, taking a seat on the end of Debbie's bed. "I knew this day would eventually come. I just didn't think it'd be this soon. "

"When's it supposed to be?" asks Bobby.

"After college, if you're lucky," replies his dad, thinking back to a slew of girlfriends in his early twenties. "So you have time to get a few practice runs in."

"Huh?"

"Listen, if you like this Chicago girl you need to tell her. That's all you can do. Cut to the chase. The truth. Otherwise, dealing with women can be downright difficult." He notices Bobby, looking out the window, lost in space. "Are you even listening to me?"

Bobby snaps out of it. "It's like there's a spotlight on her."

"And you're a mosquito, I get it."

"No, that's not, well, sort of, it's just that I blew it last night. I mean, I don't think I've got the right answer for kissing Donna."

"Slow down, you screwed up, but that's only strike one."

"Might've been strike two," Bobby informs him. "Scooter beat up her brother."

"Scooter?"

"Yeah, it was crazy."

"Okay, but are you walking back to the dugout after two strikes or are you going to stand up at the plate and take another hack?"

"I love baseball, dad, but I suck at it."

"Forget baseball," he tells Bobby. "Go win that girl back."

"Now?"

"No, you've got to come up with a plan first, a good plan." He stands and pats Bobby on the back. "And clean out the garage while you're at it."

"Today?"

"What other day is there?"

Bobby shrugs his shoulders. "All right."

"Your uncle's looking for stuff he can sell at the garage sale, maybe some of your old toys," says his dad, starting for the hallway. "And do something about your hair."

Bobby picks up his sister's hand mirror to see what's up, and for a brief moment he doesn't recognize himself. However, Bobby realizes that it's more than just the hair, that he's changed somehow, maybe even evolved. And he likes it.

Bobby puts the mirror back on Debbie's dresser and hurries after his dad to the kitchen. And, this time, he grabs a handful of sausages on his way to the basement, where Travolta waits for him, ready for a serious pow-wow. But Bobby takes one look at his idol and punches him in the head, knocking the cardboard cutout to the floor.

Later, out back by the garage, Bobby adjusts the wire coat hanger he's using as an antenna on his radio, picking up the Loop and Steve Dahl, mid-rant:

```
"I don't wanna see Margaret
Trudeau's face anymore on the
cover of anything with her little
see-through dress on, you know, or
Ali MacGraw doesn't have a bra on
and I'm not interested."
```

When Dahl's done talking he puts on "Accidents Will Happen" by Elvis Costello, just as Scooter skateboards up the driveway and ... wipes out. But he quickly dusts himself off, surprised Bobby still has his, "Rock'Em Sock'Em Robots?"

"My dad wants me to give it to my uncle," mopes Bobby, "to sell at the garage sale."

"The World's Largest Garage Sale," clarifies Scooter.

"Big deal."

"You wanna go one last round?"

"If I win," says Bobby, dead serious, "I'm keeping these guys."

Scooter puts the game down on the pavement and cracks his thumbs, getting behind the red robot. "Then you better say goodbye."

"I think not." Up for the challenge, Bobby sits on the other side of the ring and places his thumbs on the controls for the blue robot.

And they're off, hammering away at each other's heads, moving side-to-side, trying to avoid the onslaught of plastic punches until, *WHAM*, Scooter's fighter catches the blue robot right under the chin, *knocking his head off.*

"Down goes Bobby," yells Scooter. "Down goes Bobby!"

But Bobby's not impressed. "Who cares? I'm taking it back to the basement."

"I have to admit that was fun." Scooter gets up and checks out the rest of Bobby's things, starting with his baseball card collection, organized by team in a shoebox. Finding a pile of Cubs, Scooter pulls out one from 1972 and holds it up. "Check out Pepitone's sideburns," he says. "They're bigger than Carl Yastrzemski's were."

"Pepitone had cooler hair too."

"That was a wig."

"Really?" asks Bobby, somewhere between being grossed out and disillusioned.

"Yeah, it came off one time in a game."

But Bobby doesn't want to believe him. "That's a bunch of crap."

"Dude, one of my teacher's at Nichols told me Pepitone used to sell wigs in the offseason."

"I call bullshit," says Bobby, snatching the baseball card from

Scooter. "Since when have you ever listened to a teacher?"

Scooter digs through more of Bobby's stuff: Hot Wheels, marbles, his Cuddly Dudley doll. "Why're you holding on to all this?"

"Why wouldn't I?"

"It's kid stuff."

"Still, it's like my dad's trying to get rid of me or something with this whole garage sale thing."

"Don't sweat it, dude. It's just part of growing up. Like when you had to choose between the Stingray and Misty."

"But I got both."

"Not really." Scooter points to the bike in the garage, still tied to the Mercury's roof. "Tell that to your Stingray."

"I keep meaning to take it down."

"Sure."

"Well, considering Misty hates me, I suppose it's fitting."

"Give her a day to calm down," Scooter tells him. "No phone calls, no wagging tails, nothing."

"Nothing?"

"Zilch. Last night, the whole jumping on her dad's car and shit, way too intense."

"I was drunk."

"Reggie said Misty looked like one of those babes on *Soul Train*, you know, how they always have a couple of random white chicks?"

"Kind of, but way better," perks up Bobby. "No joke, she looked *dy-no-mite!*"

"Easy, J.J., I believe you."

"I goofed up, didn't I?"

"First of all, dude, you're sixteen. You don't *goof up* anything. You're not a clown, are you?"

"No."

"So relax," Scooter tells him, throwing a sympathetic arm around his buddy's shoulder. "She loves the Ramones, right?"

"Yeah."

"Then tomorrow," says Scooter, taking his arm back and giving Bobby a playful shove, "she loves you too."

The next day, Bobby follows Scooter on their skateboards up Central Street ... with no idea where he's taking them, only that Scooter thinks he knows a way to fix the rift with Misty with an assist from Joey Ramone.

Bobby pushes off on the pavement several times with his foot and catches up to Scooter, then gliding along ... notices Scooter's wearing a new t-shirt, one with the words *DISCO SUCKS!* emblazoned across the front, just like Steve Dahl's.

It's one thing when rockers like Scooter say *disco sucks*, thinks Bobby, but even worse when they have their own wardrobe. Unless, he wonders, he's been playing for the wrong team all along.

When Bobby spots the yellow and red umbrellas up ahead, his stomach knocks. Hunger? Always. Nerves? Inconveniently fraying. Bobby knows Scooter would never put Mustard's Last Stand in their path without getting something to eat.

Unless, ironically, this fast food institution is the end of the road for Bobby and Misty, where Scooter's big plan to save the summer passes the mustard so to speak or fails miserably.

As soon as they arrive out in front of Mustard's Bobby instinctively looks over his shoulder for Indians. "How is a hotdog gonna get Misty back?"

"We're not here to eat," Scooter tells him, stepping on the end of his skateboard to flip it up and grab it, cleanly. "But we can if you're starving."

"You don't want a dog?"

"I ate at your place."

"Of course." Bobby steps on his board, but it smacks him in the shin instead. "Okay, that hurt."

"Take it easy, dude." Scooter opens the door for Bobby. "Come."

Bobby limps inside Mustard's. "So if we're not eating here then what're we doing?"

Scooter leads Bobby to the counter. "Guess who's playing at Cahn on October 13th?"

"Cahn?"

"You know, where they perform Waa-mu, the theater thing at Northwestern."

"Oh, right."

"Now guess who's playing."

"Village People?" tries Bobby, wishing it was true. "Hot Chocolate?"

"Really?" Scooter asks, making sure Bobby isn't messing with him. "Think rock 'n' roll."

"Poco?"

"Poco?" Scooter's disappointed in Bobby. "You think we came all the way down to Mustard's for Poco?"

"Toto? No. Hold on just a sec. I got this." Bobby scratches his head, thinking it through. "Doobie Brothers?"

"Doobie's, yes. Brothers, no."

"The Cars?"

"That'd be cool."

"Hmm..."

"You're going about it backwards," Scooter tells him. "Who do you wanna go to a concert with?"

Bobby's brain surges with images of Misty, some he's seen, like at the pool, others he'd like to see. "You're not messing with me?" he asks, wanting the truth. "The Ramones?"

"Yeah, dude. The Ramones."

"Fuck..."

"So what're you gonna do about it?"

"I'll, uh, buy Misty and me tickets," says Bobby, coming to life. "It'll smooth things over. Has to."

"For sure."

"We'll be totally copacetic."

"Forget about it," Scooter tells him, abruptly.

"Forget about what?"

"Cahn only holds a thousand people. Show's sold-out."

"What? Why're you telling me this?" asks Bobby, deflating. "At Mustard's? When I don't have any money to get something to eat?"

"Because I've got connections." Scooter nods his head to the other side of the counter, where one of the cooks, mid-twenties, long hair pulled back in a ponytail, recognizes him.

The cook turns a row of hotdogs over on the grill and takes off his apron. "Meet me in the alley," he says, reaching for a lighter and a pack of smokes.

Bobby heads straight for the exit. He knows something's up with this guy, something that's going to help him with Misty.

Scooter watches Bobby go and smiles, hoping this will work out for his buddy. Then he catches up to him in the alley behind the restaurant, where the cook's already lighting up a cigarette like it's a breath of fresh air. "What's shakin'?" he asks the cook.

The cook holds up a pair of concert tickets and grins, one front tooth encroaching on the other. "Feast your feeble eyes on the last two tickets to see the godfathers of punk, all the way from Forest Hills Queens New York, ladies and gentlemen, I give you ... the Ramones."

Bobby can't believe his luck. "Cool!" Practically drooling, he reaches for the tickets...

But the cook pulls them back. "Not so fast," he snickers.

"Pony up."

"No problem," says Scooter, tossing him what's left of their bag of weed. "Best shit on the North Shore."

"Of Hawaii?" asks the cook, interest peeked.

"Uh..." Scooter meant, *of Chicago*, but figures he might as well go with it. "Yeah, North Shore of Hawaii."

The cook opens the bag and takes a closer look. "What's with all the seeds?" he asks, skeptically.

"I left them," replies Scooter, without missing a beat. "In case you want to grow your own."

The cook nods his head. "Righteous."

"Straight swap?" tries Scooter.

Cigarette between his lips, the cook holds the bag in one palm, the tickets in the other, weighing the value of each to his rock 'n' roll lifestyle. "Feels about right." He keeps the weed, handing Bobby the tickets.

"He shoots, he scores!" exclaims Bobby.

"Not so fast," comes a voice out of nowhere.

Bobby turns to see Woody just as he *snatches the tickets* from out of his hands. "Hey!"

"Is this what you do on your day off?" asks Woody. "Deal weed?"

"Dude," appeals Scooter, to the cook. "Can't you do something about this?"

"You cats gotta settle this elsewhere." The cook tosses his cigarette down the alley like a dart and heads back inside. "You owe me one, Woody."

"Well worth it," he smirks, starting for the Service Crew van.

But Bobby gets in his way. "Come on. Don't be a jag-off."

"What're you gonna do?" asks Woody, poking Bobby in the chest with his middle finger. "Tell your mom and dad I stole the concert tickets you bought with a bag of pot?"

"Not exactly but--"

"But nothing." Woody pushes Bobby out of the way. "And that was my bag of pot. I'm not stupid." He gets in the van and makes a show of it as he speeds off, the tires kicking up gravel...

Bobby looks to Scooter, pissed. "Are we gonna just let him go?"

"Come on, I'll buy you a dog."

"What? Those tickets were for Misty."

"Are you hungry or not?"

"Yeah," moans Bobby. "But what the fuck? I needed those tickets."

"Take a chill pill," says Scooter, leading them back into Mustard's. "At least we know who has 'em."

Chapter 8

ROCK LOBSTER

The very next night Bobby parks the Mercury on Sheridan Road, across from a handful of big brick houses known as Northwestern's fraternity Row. The four boys are in their usual spots in the stationwagon. No one has to ask anyone to *slide over*. No has to yell out *shotgun*. These boys just fit together. A crew in the making. A summer to remember. If only they could figure out what to do.

"Why'd you pull over?" wonders Tim, scarfing down a bag of Doritos in the back. "At NU?"

"Are you gonna share those things or not?" asks Bobby, a little testy.

"You stopped for chips?" wonders Tim, still munching away.

Resting peacefully in the middle seat, Reggie reluctantly sits up and snatches the bag from Tim. "You heard the man." He finds the last couple of chips at the bottom of the bag and hands it to Scooter. "Good luck."

"I don't need luck." Scooter tips the bag upside down into his mouth, relishing every last crumb... "I make it."

"That's great," says Reggie, not wanting to get Scooter started on a tangent. "But why'd we stop? Is there a movie at Tech?"

"Good question," begins Scooter, nonchalantly throwing the

bag of Doritos out the window. "Tonight, however--"

"Why'd you do that?" interrupts Bobby.

"Do what?" asks Scooter, innocently.

"That," replies Bobby, pointing out the window. "With the bag."

"It was empty," says Scooter. "Trust me."

"So you just tossed it on the ground?"

"I didn't think you'd want me to leave it in your dad's car."

"You're right," confirms Bobby, nodding his head excessively. "I don't. I want you to get rid of it like any other normal human being--in a garbage can."

Scooter shakes his head. "You are such a girl."

Bobby turns around to plead his case to Tim and Reggie. "Come on, you guys've seen that commercial with the Indian, you know, where he's standing on the side of the road crying?"

"The one where he's hitchhiking?" asks Reggie, pretending not to know.

"What? No. He's not hitchhiking," clarifies Bobby. "He's just standing there checking things out."

"Sounds suspicious," says Tim.

"Why do I even bother?" Bobby throws his hands up in the air in disgust. "Don't you know we're destroying our planet."

But Scooter isn't overly concerned. "The earth will survive," he says. "It's the human species that needs to be worried."

"I'm down with that," says Reggie.

Tim too, in his own way. "One of the O'Hollearns said the Indian guy in the commercial is just an actor, that he's actually Italian."

"Who listens to any of the O'Hollearns?" asks Bobby, incredulously.

"The sister's supposedly smart," says Reggie, laying back down in the middle seat.

"Whatever, first Pepitone's wearing a wig and now the Indian," rants Bobby. "Why do you guys have to ruin everything for me?"

"Ruin?" repeats Scooter. "More like educate."

"So you're telling me that being a litterbug is a sign of intelligence?" asks Bobby.

"Just an Italian litterbug," he replies, "in a wig."

"Would you two pipe down?" butts in Tim. "You still haven't told us why we're here."

"Yeah," says Reggie. "I was under the impression that we had something to do tonight. Something important."

"We do," starts Scooter, packing a small wooden pipe with weed. "You see, we're all sixteen now. We're men. And life for a man, well, it's about women. You see--"

"How long is this gonna take?" interjects Tim. "I gotta pee."

"Look," continues Scooter, "the short of it is that women provide food, sex, offspring, all that shit."

"I think the guy's supposed to get the food," says Reggie. "You know, hunt for it."

"Okay," allows Scooter. "But she cooks it. And in return, all women want is money. Or at least all that money can buy, right? Like when Bobby's dad, didn't you find it strange when he got Barbara that mink coat, what was it, three weeks *after* Christmas?"

"I asked you guys not to call my mom by her first name?" complains Bobby. "It's kind of creepy."

"It's for story purposes only," lies Scooter. "Point is, Barbara was totally stoked. Still, you could tell your dad was making up for some previous infraction, like the mink had magic powers and shit."

"Since when are you paying so much attention to my parents relationship?" asks Bobby, a bit baffled.

"I don't know," replies Scooter, "just seems like everybody's parents are getting divorced lately."

"So you guys drove us here to talk about divorce?" wonders Tim.

"Or money?" asks Reggie.

"Not exactly," begins Scooter again. "To make a long story a little less long, we know that the four of us don't have the money to buy our girlfriends, or potential girlfriends, mink coats. But what we do have is the advantage of being able to get them something money can't buy when your sixteen."

"A house?" tries Reggie.

Tim holds up his hand. "Blackhawk tickets?"

"No, though Hawks tickets can be hard to come by," admits Scooter. "Anyway, sixteen-year-old girls can't get booze."

"Unless they wait outside a liquor store," says Tim, "and try to get someone to buy it for them."

"Or call a cab and ask for a delivery," adds Reggie. "I just tell 'em it's for my grams."

"Let me clarify," says Scooter. "Sixteen-year-old girls can't score *a lot* of booze. And a lot of booze is much more fun than a little booze." Scooter points to the frat houses across the street. "Which brings us to Beta."

Tim takes off his Cub hat and rubs his scalp. "I don't get it."

"Me neither," admits Bobby. "Unless you're talking about Woody."

"Yup," confirms Scooter. "He's a Beta down at Southern. The fuck's been hanging out here all summer."

Reggie sits up again, interested. "So?"

"So tonight," replies Scooter, putting the pipe in his pocket, "the brothers are throwing a little summer set."

"We're gonna crash Woody's party?" asks Tim.

"No," replies Scooter. "We're gonna *take* his party."

"Take his party?" repeats Reggie for clarification.

"How're we even gonna get in?" asks Tim.

"Woody knows Bobby wants those tickets," says Scooter. "He's pretty much expecting us. He's just not expecting what we're gonna do if he doesn't give them back." Scooter gets out of the car and picks up the bag of Doritos.

"What happened to the pipe?" asks Reggie.

"That's all the weed we've got left," replies Scooter.

"So let's smoke it," says Tim. "I can't party once football practice starts."

"And I respect that," says Scooter. "But you shouldn't smoke your last bowl until you've found your next one. You never know if it'll come in handy."

"Words of weed wisdom," jokes Reggie. "Is someone taking notes?"

"You probably should," says Scooter. "Now follow me. I've got a plan."

Scooter leads the boys through the front door of the Beta house, nice and easy, like he owns the place, a brave move if anyone inside had cared to notice. A stack of speakers in front of the living room fireplace blasts The B-52's "Rock Lobster," a song the boys have never heard before but will practically become their theme song by the end of the summer; a kooky, new-wave cat-call to just about everything and nothing at all in a sonic mix of Egyptian keyboards and surf guitars.

A strobe light reveals a burly Beta dancing by himself, drunk, bordering on sloppy, entertaining a gaggle of nerdy Northwestern girls ready to make a break for the school library. The boys move on to the dining room, or mess hall, where a fresh-faced Beta in a polo and corduroys tries to keep up behind a bar overflowing with fellow students, mostly amped-up Betas playing Ro-Sham-Bo and punching each other in the arm.

When they reach the stairs Scooter tells the boys to, "Spread out."

While The B-52's Fred Schneider sings something about a *"potion in the ocean,"* the boys take off in different directions, making their way through the fraternity house. Basement, kitchen, den, it's not exactly packed since it's summer break.

As a result, Bobby's feeling brave and makes it all the way to the third floor, poking his head in the occasional open door for Woody. But so far it's just been a lot of empty bunk-beds, one very tired foosball table, and a few Playboy centerfolds taped to a mirror, including Candy Loving and Miss May, Michelle Drake, already a favorite of Bobby's.

Bobby finds another door ajar and is all set on taking a peek inside the room, when he runs head on into a Beta walking out.

"What're you doing up here?" the Beta wants to know, sticking his chest out like he knows where NU's weight room is.

"Nothing," replies Bobby, doing an about-face. "Just looking for a beer."

The Beta grabs his shoulder, spinning him back around. "This party is for bros only, kid."

Bobby was about to make a run for it, but he's offended. "I'm not a kid."

"Whatever. No locals."

"I'm with Woody," tries Bobby. "He invited me."

"Yeah, okay, I know Woody," concedes the Beta. "He'll vouch for you?"

"Sure."

"Because he owes me a ton of weed."

"Bummer," sympathizes Bobby.

"Huh?" The Beta doesn't like the sound of that. "How well do you know Woody?"

"Uh..." Bobby quickly backtracks. "You know."

"No, I don't."

"Neither do I," shrugs Bobby. "You haven't seen him tonight, have you?"

But the Beta ignores the question and turns back into his room. "Don't push your luck," he says, closing the door.

Bobby breathes a sigh of relief when a couple of college girls barge past him down the hall on a mission with none other than Scooter following close behind...

"They just tapped a new keg on the second floor," Scooter tells him. "Come."

Glad to see a familiar face, Bobby trails Scooter down the stairs to a large gym-like bathroom, where one of the college girls is already pumping the tap on a keg in a shower stall as her friend pours each of them a beer into plastic cups.

Bobby's certain these two girls could take Scooter and him in a fight. Why he's sizing them up though, he isn't sure. But one of them has thunder thighs and a *Northwestern Field Hockey* t-shirt camouflaging an intimidating rack, surely a *Mc--* before her name or a *--ski* after, while her friend, the one on the tap, has arms that would make a bear jealous.

Thunder Thighs chugs her entire beer in one long gulp, then comes up for air. "You two look kind of young," she says, eying the boys as if they might be the main course.

"Better than kind of old," tries Scooter.

The girls laugh, perhaps with him, probably at him, taking their time as they fill each of their beers back to the brim and leave.

Before they're even out of sight, Reggie shows up, from the other end of the hall, removing bedsheet after bedsheet from underneath his shirt with a big grin on his face.

Bobby looks from Reggie to Scooter, beads of sweat gathering on his forehead. "You guys can't be serious?"

Scooter holds out his hand. "Gimme the keys to the Mercury."

"What about Woody?" wonders Bobby. "We haven't even asked him for the tickets yet."

"As far as I can tell," says Scooter, "he's not here."

"Me too," Reggie informs him. "I looked everywhere."

"Okay, but couldn't we just hang?" proposes Bobby. "Have a couple of beers? Wouldn't that be revenge enough?"

"We're sticking to the plan," says Reggie, tying the ends of the sheets together to form a rope. "Tim's already down there."

Bobby looks out the bathroom window and sees Tim, two floors below them along the side of the house.

"The idea is to not leave empty handed," continues Reggie.

"Sometimes," explains Scooter. "You just gotta skip plan A and move on to plan B."

Reggie ties the last of the bedsheets around his waist. "Especially when plan B involves getting the fuck outta Dodge."

"Fine." Bobby hands Scooter the car keys. "What do you want me to do?"

"I told you. You're the guard," says Scooter. "Just make sure no one comes in here."

"Okay." Bobby watches Scooter bolt down the stairs and then turns his attention back to Reggie, who's wrapping the other end of the sheets around the keg. "How's it going?"

"Almost done."

Bobby thinks it might be a good idea to close the bathroom door and, just as he does, turns back into the hallway to find, "Woody."

"What're you doing here?" asks Woody, trying to get around him. "Get outta my way."

But Bobby doesn't back down and gives it the old college try. "I, uh, I want my Ramones tickets back."

"And I want my weed back," counters Woody. "I know that

wasn't all of it yesterday."

"Your weed?" bluffs Bobby. "That was some of Reggie's cousin's stash. You know, the one who set all those records in track at Evanston--in the shot put."

But Woody's not buying it. "I thought that cat was in jail."

"You're right. He was," acknowledges Bobby. "Besides, how could I steal your shit? I've never even been to your frat before."

"Still playing stupid," says Woody, shaking his head. "And I can appreciate that. But if you want to see the Ramones, you better cough up my weed. Now step aside. I need a beer."

But Bobby holds fast at the door. "Those're my tickets."

"I don't care," snarls Woody, just inches from Bobby's face. "Move."

"Actually, a couple of girls are in there using the toilets," lies Bobby, finding it not only intimidating but weird to have Woody so close to him. "I, uh, promised they could have some privacy."

"How noble of you," says Woody, when a girl, a bit disheveled, snuggles up behind him, kissing him on the neck.

"I'm thirsty," she tells Woody sweetly, like she's earned it.

But Woody ignores her, choosing instead to stare down Bobby. "Don't even think about telling your sister."

Bobby knows he has him in a pickle and shoots for the moon one last time. "Tickets."

"Nice try," says Woody, sideswiping past him into the bathroom to find Reggie, who's leaning hard against the wall, *slowly lowering the keg out the second story window...*

By the time Reggie spots Woody he's been punched in the face, still somehow managing to steady the keg while yelling at Bobby to, "Go!"

With Woody focused on Reggie, Bobby kicks him in the ass and tries to shove him inside a stall, then bails down the hallway, down the stairs, and outside...

Where Tim waits underneath the window for the keg, which Reggie has lowered to within a few feet of his outstretched arms, despite Woody trying to strangle him.

"That's it, keep it coming," yells Tim, reaching for the keg as he flings off his Cub hat to get a better look, like a catcher tossing aside his mask to catch a pop foul.

Meanwhile, Bobby heads straight for Tim, his eyes glued on the fight up in the bathroom. "We got trouble!"

Woody punches Reggie in the back of the head, almost propelling him out the window, forcing Reggie to let go of the last sheet just to defend himself.

Now loose, the keg *drops...*

"I got it!" screams Bobby, *running straight into Tim*, knocking both boys off their feet and crashing to the ground--with the keg landing on top of them.

Dazed and confused, they look up just in time to see Reggie leap from the window like the Six Million Dollar Man, only he hits the ground more like himself, rolling his ankle.

Woody leans out the window, screaming his head off and waving his fist around, which is disturbing, thinks Bobby, but of no immediate danger.

That is until Woody points out their position to an angry mob of Betas storming out of the house...

Despite it weighing a ton, Tim snaps to action and throws the keg over his shoulder, while Bobby gets Reggie up, helping him take the pressure off his ankle; the three of them hobbling and wobbling as fast as they can toward Sheridan Road...

With seven or eight drunk, enraged, and possibly sexually frustrated Betas, ready to pummel the boys, maybe even paddle them.

Fortunately, Scooter's waiting along the curb in the Mercury with the engine revving and doors open.

Reggie dives into the backseat, grabbing his throbbing ankle, just as Bobby hip-checks Reggie's door closed and hops in front with Scooter, out of breath but ready for takeoff.

But Tim's not quite there yet. He couldn't keep up, not with the keg, which allows one of the Betas to break free of the pack and gain valuable ground on him...

It's not a Beta though; it's Thunder Thighs from the upstairs bathroom, running after Tim like he stole her virginity...

Tim barely beats her to the Mercury, quickly rolling the keg off his shoulder through the back window. Then he jumps up on the fender and grabs ahold of the Stingray, which is still tied to the roof, slapping the side of the car like a cowboy for Scooter to, "Hit it!"

Unfortunately for Tim, Thunder Thighs *leaps for his legs...* Unfortunately for Thunder Thighs, she misses and eats pavement as Scooter steps on the gas, honks the horn, and flips on the radio, just in time to hear David Lee Roth start singing about getting out on your own and going for it, but being prepared to pay a price:

> I live my life like there's no tomorrow
> And all I've got, I had to steal
> Least I don't need to beg or borrow
> Yes I'm livin' at a pace that kills
>
> --Van Halen

Scooter parks the Mercury in the alley behind Tim's house before "Runnin' With The Devil" even ends, allowing Tim to jump off the fender and grab a few cups from the garage.

"Where's your Cub hat?" asks Scooter, when he returns to unload the keg.

"At Beta," Tim replies, bitterly.

"Forget it," urges Scooter, pouring each of them a beer in the alley. "That hat is long gone."

"Going back is too risky," adds Reggie. "We barely made it out of there alive tonight."

"No kidding," sighs Bobby.

"Dudes..." Scooter raises his cup, a sly grin sneaking across his face. "Cheers to being alive."

"And thanks for going over there with me," says Bobby, raising his cup to the boys. "I mean, I didn't get the tickets but, you know, you had my back. Cheers."

Reggie meets their cups with his. "Fuck those guys."

"Cheers," joins in Tim, even if he does so somewhat reluctantly. "But I still want my hat back," he says. "I've had that thing my whole life."

"You've got to let go," says Scooter.

"Why would you let go of something you love?" asks Tim.

"So if it doesn't come back," he replies, "you'll know it wasn't meant to be."

"Check out Scooter," laughs Reggie, "getting all philosophical and shit."

"More like, *and shit*," says Tim, downing the rest of his beer.

Scooter ignores Tim and takes his cup, refilling it for him. "If it's okay with your parents, Timmy, we should leave the car here tonight. Otherwise, Woody's gonna end up at Bobby's house lookin' for trouble."

"Sounds good to me," says Bobby.

"What're you gonna tell your dad?" asks Reggie, leaning up against the car to take the pressure off his ankle.

"I'll tell him the truth," replies Bobby. "I had a beer and walked home."

Scooter freshens up Bobby's cup. "Make that two."

"Thanks." Bobby kneels down and gets a closer look at Reggie's ankle, then up at Tim. "Got any ice inside?"

"Sure," says Tim, heading toward the house...

"Bring a bunch of it," Scooter tells him. "We should try and keep the keg cool."

"What if Woody comes over here looking for it?" asks Reggie, still concerned.

"He won't come near this place," replies Scooter. "Not after he kicked one of Tim's brothers off Clark Street beach for not having a token. I think it was Nick. The one that plays hockey at Madison. Anyway, Woody escorted him off the beach in front of a bunch of chicks. Totally embarrassed him."

"The girls were supposedly super hot too," chimes in Bobby, "from Niles West or North or something."

"And really tan," adds Scooter.

"Is that all you cats can think about?" asks Reggie. "Girls?"

"That's easy for you to say," claims Bobby. "You've got Patti."

"True, but it's not just Woody," worries Reggie. "We've got an entire fraternity mad at us."

"Don't forget the girls field hockey team," says Scooter.

Bobby looks at Reggie, shaking his head in disbelief. "I can't believe you jumped out the window."

"I didn't have much of a choice," says Reggie. "Two other Betas ran in. It was like fighting a ceiling fan. *Bam Bam Bam.*" He smiles, revealing blood-stained teeth. "I got a couple good licks in though."

Bobby gets a closer look at Reggie's battered face. "I think we're gonna have black eye number three tomorrow morning."

"Can black people even get black eyes?" asks Scooter.

"Shut up," Reggie tells him. "My mother's gonna kill me if I come home looking like this."

DISCO INFERNO!

"Maybe you can spend the night at Tim's," suggests Scooter.

"And maybe, just maybe, we should quit stealing things," says Bobby.

"Like I said..." Scooter tops everyone's beer. "You can't call it stealing, if you can't buy it."

Bobby takes a sip of his beer. "I'll never get used to that idea but it almost makes sense."

"Man," sighs Reggie. "You cats are crazy." He takes off a sneaker to get a better look at his ankle. "All over some random redhead from Chicago."

"Who's a Sox fan," Scooter reminds them.

"The Sox thing I can't help but she's not some random chick," counters Bobby. "Besides, how many times do I have say I just wanted my bike back."

"Which is why it's still on the roof," points out Reggie.

"I already told him that," says Scooter. "Yesterday."

Bobby starts to untie his bike. "I'll ride home."

"What're we gonna do about this keg?" asks Tim, walking in with a couple of ice trays. "My brothers are bound to sniff this thing out before long."

"The Ramones tickets would've been a nice touch, but I was thinkin' we'd take the keg to the South Side as a peace offering," replies Scooter. "See if Bobby can make up with Misty."

"You've got to be shitting me," moans Tim.

"Nope." Scooter lights another scrunched up cigarette and looks to Bobby. "At least me and lover boy are going."

Bobby lifts his bike down from the roof of the stationwagon and gives it the once-over. "In all honesty, I think this is one of those nothing to lose, everything to gain situations."

"And I think," says Reggie, holding a couple of ice cubes to his ankle, "this is one of those situations where whoever's in love shouldn't call the shots."

"He lost me after *in all honesty*," says Tim.

Scooter blows a convincing puff of smoke into the rafters. "We're doin' it."

"I can't believe my ears," says Reggie. "Hanging out with you guys almost makes me wish school would start up again.

Chapter 9

RENEGADE

Debbie drags a suitcase into the kitchen the next morning and stops in front of Bobby, who's sitting at the table hunched over a plate of scrambled eggs, pretending to be interested in the morning paper.

"Hey," she says, already irritated with him.

Bobby pokes his nose around the Sun-Times to make sure Woody isn't lurking and spots her suitcase. "Where're you going?"

"Up to Fox Lake," she replies, eating the eggs off his plate with her fingers. "To stay with Gram."

Bobby senses something is off with his sister and gets up, preferring to be a moving target. "Oh, I thought we were all going together this weekend."

"Obviously not. Do you know where dad's car is?" she asks. "Mom said he took the train in to work."

"Dad's car?" stalls Bobby, knowing all roads lead back to Woody.

"Yeah."

Heike trots in waving her long brown nose around ... sensing danger.

Bobby sticks his head inside the fridge, like he can't find what he wants. "I can pick it up for you," he tells her, thinking up a lie, face-to-face with a head of lettuce. "It's up on Green Bay Road.

Oil change."

"Doesn't Dad normally do that?"

"He puts oil in it," explains Bobby, unsure if Debbie's on to him. "He doesn't change it."

Debbie sighs, her distress filling the room, and slumps down at the table in Bobby's chair. "Me and Woody broke up last night."

Bobby's happy for her. "That's good news, kind of, right?" He grabs the orange juice out of the fridge just to keep busy and pours himself a glass.

"I know you stole his pot, Bobby."

He quickly hands her the juice, hoping to keep things civil. "So why didn't you say anything?"

"Because he blamed me. Said I threw it away, until your little run-in at Mustard's."

"Yeah, got screwed out of some Ramones tickets," laments Bobby. "That was a drag."

"No kidding, you got set up."

"Kind of figured that when the guy knew Woody's name."

"He's always pulling stunts like that. Whatever or whoever it takes." Debbie rests her chin in her hand. "We went out for two years," she says, a lone tear escaping down her cheek, which she quickly smothers with the back of her hand. "I always knew he was kind of a dickhead. It's just that, until now, he was never a dickhead to me." Debbie begins picking at Bobby's eggs again, this time with his fork. "Can I have some toast?"

"Yeah, sure, of course," says Bobby, putting two slices of white bread in the toaster. "If it makes you feel any better, I saw Woody with a girl last night."

"You what?" Debbie hastily washes a mouthful of eggs down with the juice. "Where?"

"At the Beta House," he replies, wishing he hadn't brought it up.

"Wow, and here he was making me out to be the bad guy."

"I'm sorry, Debs. I know you liked him."

"I did," she says. "But now I think I hate him too."

"Welcome to the club."

"There's a club?" jokes Debbie.

"Should be."

"I can't believe he invited you to one of their parties."

"He didn't exactly invite us," admits Bobby. "We just sort've popped by."

"And you saw the girl? No wonder he didn't say anything about running into you."

"Get this though, we stole one of their kegs," says Bobby proudly. "The tap too."

"Huh?"

"Probably killed the whole party."

Debbie stops eating. "Have you lost your mind?"

"What? It's just beer."

"No, it isn't. That's not it. Last couple days or so you're different somehow..." She looks her baby brother up and down. "You haven't combed your hair. You've got a wicked shiner. And you've been in my room listening to songs about chicken vindaloo and being sedated. Hold it. It's a girl, isn't't?"

"Jeez-Louise," says Bobby, throwing his hands up in the air. "Is it that obvious?"

"Your first serious girlfriend," smiles Debbie.

"I wish," admits Bobby. "But at this particular moment I don't even think we're friends."

"Bummer, little brother."

"Now that you know, don't you have some advice for me?" asks Bobby. "Dad did."

"Okay, take it easy, loverboy." Debbie finishes the eggs and drinks the last of the juice, giving her brother's situation some thought. "You know what?"

"What?"

"Love stinks."

"Really? Love stinks? That's all you've got for me?"

"No, there's more." Debbie gets up from the table and heads back upstairs...

Bobby just stands there scratching his head until she returns and hands him a record album, the cover of which is four close-up pictures of the same white guy and his brown beard.

"If you're listening to rock," says Debbie, "not to mention dating, you're gonna need a little Van Morrison."

"Van Morrison?" he asks, having never heard of him before. "Is he related to Van Halen?"

"I wouldn't think so." Debbie grabs a piece of bread out of the toaster and picks up her suitcase. "Start with the second song, side one," she says, leaving out the back door. "I'll drive the Rabbit up to Fox Lake."

Bobby takes Misty's boot over to Vose Bootery, a shoe store up on Central Street where he got his first pair of Keds, and later, a pair of Topsiders for middle school at Haven. And though the store specializes in selling kid shoes, he's hoping the owner can help him fix the heel on the boot. Meanwhile, that guy with the beard, his song is already stuck in Bobby's head:

> Well, it's a marvelous night for a moondance
> With the stars up above in your eyes
> A fantabulous night to make romance
> 'Neath the cover of October skies

> --Van Morrison

Bobby sets the boot and the heel on the counter, waiting for someone to notice him, humming along to a song no one else can hear, when an older man comes out of the back room, carrying a box of shoes.

"Well hello there, Bobby," he says, recognizing him. "What've you got there?"

"It broke," Bobby feels the need to clarify.

"Is this Barbara's?" he asks.

"No, it's, you know," mumbles Bobby, still getting used to the idea of discussing his love life with everyone. "It belongs to a girl ... friend. I hope."

"Ahh, I see," says the man, winking at him. "She got the legs to put in a fancy boot like this?"

"Yeah, they work."

The man laughs, realizing Bobby isn't in on the joke, and gets to the point. "I don't normally work on shoes," he explains. "I just sell them."

"Please," Bobby practically begs. "She's mad at me and I don't know what else to do and--"

"Okay, hold your horses." The man removes his glasses, getting a closer look at where the heel broke off. "Let me see what I can do."

"Thanks," says Bobby, shaking his hand. "Thank you."

"Don't thank me yet," he cautions. Still, he appreciates Bobby's enthusiasm. "Come back around this afternoon."

Bobby walks outside with a bounce in his step, already dreaming of a chocolate éclair from down the street at Tag's Bakery. Happy, he decides to introduce his favorite new word to the scorching July sun, "*Fantabulous.*"

Later that day, after pacing the kitchen floor for close to an hour and completely confusing Heike, Bobby finally summons the courage to call Misty's house. But first, he wants a glass of milk, then quickly realizes he's just stalling again. He pulls the scrap of paper out of his pocket that Misty gave him that first night on the South Side and picks up the phone, staring at her number, but only dials it in his head.

"Just call her," says Bobby's mother, passing through the kitchen to grab her tennis racket.

"I don't know what you're talking about," tries Bobby.

"You should've stuck with Donna."

"How do you know who I'm calling?"

"I'm your mother," she replies. "I know everything."

"Well then does Chicago have a different area code than us?"

"We're all 312," she says on her way out the screen door. "I'll be at the park if you need me. I'm going to get revenge for losing to Mrs. DeStefano on the 4th."

When he's sure his mom is gone, Bobby chucks caution to the wind and dials Misty's number on the rotary telephone... pulling the chord down the basement steps for some privacy.

"Hello, hi," starts Bobby, eagerly waiting for the sound of her voice.

"You got some nerve."

It's not who he was hoping for. "Is Misty there?"

Over in Bridgeport, Ian's melting into the living room couch, trying to ignore the heat by watching *Gilligan's Island* on TV. He hangs the phone up on that Evanston shit without giving it a second thought and adjusts a fan so that it's pointing directly at him.

Bobby dials her number again, one finger at a time... "Hey, Ian. I think we got disconnected."

Ian listens half-heartedly, wondering whether Gilligan's going to screw up another golden opportunity to get everyone off that damn island. And better yet, if they are stuck, who's the Professor going to bang first, Ginger or Mary Ann? He hangs up again.

Bobby takes a deep breath and dials her number once more... "Can I please talk to your sister?"

"Who said she's even home?"

"Hey, I know you and me, we've had our differences but can you at least tell her I'm on the line?"

"Nah." Ian hangs up a third time.

Pissed, Bobby quickly calls back, his fingers getting sore from spinning the dial... "Don't hang up on me, dude."

"Who're you callin' dude?" asks Misty's dad, on the other end this time.

"Oh, shit, I mean, shoot, sir," stammers Bobby. "Sorry, is your car okay?"

"Boy, just so you know, I don't like you."

"Please, sir," tries Bobby. "May I speak with your daughter?"

"Look..." sighs her dad, caving just a little. "I doubt she ever wants to talk to you again, but even if she did, she's at work."

Bobby hasn't a clue where Misty works, so he sets a trap. "At the whatchamacallit?"

"Yeah, the roller rink," he unwittingly reveals. "So don't bother her."

"Wouldn't think of it," lies Bobby, hanging up.

That night, Bobby throws on Debbie's Aerosmith t-shirt and sets off to retrieve his dad's Mercury from Tim's garage, telling his parents he wouldn't be long. However, Bobby has convinced the boys to drive with him, yet again, deep into Chicago. And they've done that. But as far as the mission goes, they're not having much luck.

"How many roller rinks are there on the South Side?" asks Tim, growing weary.

"Yeah," yawns Reggie. "Couldn't we have just played Space

135

Invaders at the Spot?"

"Hold on..." Scooter flips through an enormous phone book until he finds the page he's looking for. "This is the last one," he tells them. "Bobby, turn right on Archer."

"It's probably closed by now," says Tim, steadying the keg in the back.

But Bobby pulls into the parking lot of the Fleetwood Skating Rink. "Let's just give it a try." He parks the car and runs up to the entrance, knocking impatiently on the glass doors, which are locked, while the neon sign above him shuts off. Dejected, Bobby turns to leave...

When Misty opens the door in her satin *Fleetwood* jacket, trying a little too hard to act like she doesn't care that Bobby's just showed up out of the blue at her job. "What do you want?"

"Still open?" tries Bobby, holding up his roller skates.

"You're too late," she replies, without sympathy.

Tim lugs the keg to the front door anyway. "Where do you want this?"

"What's that for?" asks Misty.

"Drinking," replies Scooter, getting out of the car.

"And it's heavy," adds Tim, looking from Bobby to Misty. "So sort your shit out."

Mary walks up behind her, also in a *Fleetwood* jacket, getting a load of the boys--and the beer. "We can stay open a little longer."

Misty gives her the evil eye.

"What?" asks Mary. "I mean, if they came all this way to skate."

The Fleetwood is empty except for Misty, Mary, and the manager; a pretty woman in her early thirties, fighting off the temptation to act like a teenager with her two young coworkers. Still, her hair is dyed pink. She's overdosed on eyeliner. And she hasn't come to terms with the end of the 60's. But who could blame her? Candice is a perfect mix of blue-collar and hippie. Urban and hardworking as they come but game for a weekend camping trip.

Done for the night, Candace lights a cigarette, scrutinizing the boys as they lace up their roller skates (except for Reggie who's on crutches). This Bobby kid is cute, she thinks. He has warm blue eyes. And he brought his own pair of skates. She looks over at Mary, circling the rink with a giant broom. Bobby's not her type, thinks Candice, too nice. But she knows Misty's different. To her, boys can never be too nice.

"Lock up when you're through," she tells Misty, tossing her the keys. "And watch out for the good-looking one."

"Of course." Misty trusts Candice's intuition when it comes to men, especially since she's never married. "I don't even like him."

"That's when the trouble starts," laughs Candice. "And don't stay here to some ungodly hour."

"Right."

"Keep the lights down too."

"We got it, Candice." Mary returns to make sure she's leaving. "Thanks."

"And don't let those boys spill any of that Schlitz on my wood floors," she warns the girls.

"The keg, it's Pabst," says Mary. "I've already had a cup."

Candice shakes her head. "Just keep your legs closed, will ya?"

"Come on, how much trouble can we get in?" jokes Mary. "They're just a bunch of pussies from Evanston."

"Just... You know," says Candice. "And pour me a beer to go."

"I'll get you one." Misty puts the keys in the door and heads for the keg.

In the meantime, Mary wants to get this party started and

looks through a stack of records, just as the boys take to the rink on roller skates... Immediately, Scooter struggles to stay upright, like it's his first time, while Tim, on the other hand, flies around the rink, mostly because he plays hockey.

Then there's Bobby, completely at ease, having perfected his skills on wheels at roller rinks closer to Evanston like the Rainbo in Uptown, the Playdium in Glenview, and the Axle over in Niles.

Mary finally finds a record she thinks will get the biggest rise of out Misty and puts it on, cranking "Miss You" from a couple of speakers suspended over the rink (the eight minute, 12-inch version), the closest the Rolling Stones have come to a disco song.

Bobby gets a burst of energy from Mick and the lads that has him skating backwards and crisscrossing his feet while flapping his elbows like a chicken...

> Well, I've been haunted in my sleep
> You've been starring in my dreams
> Lord, I miss you
>
> --The Rolling Stones

And Bobby's quite pleased with himself until he notices that Misty isn't paying any attention to him, focusing instead on a pinball machine in the back corner, smacking and shaking a Bally, the Elton John *Capt. Fantastic* one, where Elton is wearing the huge sunglasses, skullcap, and suspenders.

But Bobby isn't giving up on Misty. Not even. He skates right over to the keg and, pumping the tap a few times, pours a beer. Then he skates it over to Misty, setting the cup on top of the pinball machine.

"Don't put it there," she tells him, without taking her eyes off the pinball.

"Sorry," apologizes Bobby, taking the beer back. "It's for

you."

Misty's on a roll though and keeps on playing. "I can pour my own," she says, racking up point after point.

But Bobby persists, nodding at the picture of Elton on the machine. "My sister has this album."

Misty ignores him, at least on the outside.

"That song, the one with sugar bears and butterflies and people getting woken up at four in the morning, used to make me, I don't know, sad."

"It's a break-up song," she tells him, void of emotion.

"Oh... I'm, uh, really sorry about the other night. Really. I mean it."

"What do I care?"

Bobby takes a deep breath and a sip of the beer. "That whole thing with Donna was a giant misunderstanding."

"A misunderstanding? You were making out with her."

"Actually she just sort of grabbed me and kissed me and I was drunk and didn't think you were coming."

"So you're some kind of lush?"

"No."

Misty slaps the side of the machine as the ball gets by her flippers and down the hole. She finally turns to Bobby, laying it all out. "I felt so stupid."

"What? Why?"

"All those girls in their fancy dresses. Why'd you even invite me?"

"Because I like you. And I want to hang out with you. And every time we start to kiss we get interrupted by Scooter or your brother or whatever."

"So maybe we shouldn't kiss any more. Maybe we just weren't meant to be."

"There's only one way to find out." Bobby moves in close for a kiss...

But she cuts him off. "Nice try."

"So that's it?"

Misty isn't sure. "How's your head?"

"My head?"

"You know, your head, my dad's windshield, up close and personal."

"Oh, it's okay. Just a little bump."

"My dad's still pissed."

"I take it you are too."

"I don't know," she says. "I thought it was funny."

"Funny?"

"Yeah, not so much when it happened but the next day... I guess I realized how much you cared."

"So what do we do?"

"We get my skates on," says Misty, taking the beer from him. "I never get a chance when I'm working."

"Cool, lemme grab a record from my car."

"It better be good," she tells him as he skates out the front door. "I have a reputation around here."

With Candice gone, Mary and the boys have gravitated to the keg and a game of quarters, while Misty sits at the edge of the rink, tying up her roller skates; a white pair adorned with orange wheels, orange laces, and orange pom-poms. Once she's ready, she waits for Bobby who hands his record off to Mary and skates up to her, holding something behind his back.

"Is that the album cover?" asks Misty.

"Nope." He shows her. "Your boot." And hands it to her.

"You're kidding?"

"I had it fixed."

Misty looks it over. "That was sweet of you," she tells him, then gets all quiet, struggling with her words. "Those... It's gonna sound stupid but ... those were my mom's boots."

"She gave them to you?"

"Not exactly, she..."

Bobby can sense something's wrong. "We don't have to talk about it if you don't want to."

"No, I do," she says, turning away. "Just not now."

"Okay." Bobby tries to lighten the mood. "Hey, Mary," he calls out to her. "What happened to my record?"

Mary downs the rest of her beer. "I got it."

"Side one," he continues.

"Relax." She walks over to the turntable, stopping to shine the spotlight on the floor as Bobby and Misty begin to skate around the rink.

Bobby, perhaps overly excited, tells Misty, "I got us concert tickets."

"Us?"

"Yeah."

"Shouldn't you have asked me first?"

"Nah."

"We don't even like the same music."

"So you don't want to see the Ramones?"

"Are you shitting me? The Ramones? At Northwestern?"

"October 13th."

"That's so cool. My dad doesn't have any pull in Evanston."

"That's okay," smiles Bobby. "I do."

"No shit?"

"Yeah, can you go?"

"For sure, but the Ramones? That's kind of different for you, isn't it?"

"So are you." Bobby takes her hand as the music kicks in, Van Morrison's "And It Stoned Me" from his sister's *Moondance* album:

> And it stoned me to my soul
> Stoned me just like jelly roll
> And it stoned me
>
> --Van Morrison

"Nice song!" shouts out Reggie.

Scooter stands on a table. "Let's get stoned!"

"Scooter's crazy," smiles Misty.

"In a good way," says Bobby.

"Yeah."

"So maybe we could get together sometime between now and October."

Misty squeezes his hand. "What're you doing tomorrow?"

And Bobby squeezes back. "Something with you I hope."

"It's Disco Demolition Night."

"I know."

"Does that mean you're going?" she asks, pulling Bobby over to the side of the rink.

"I want to." Bobby leans in again for a kiss but as usual with them it's disrupted, this time by flashing lights.

"Mary!" complains Misty. "Would you turn those lights off?"

"It's not me," she says, peeking out a window.

"Who is it then?" asks Misty.

"Cherry tops." Mary looks at the boys. "Get the keg out the back door."

The boys quickly grab the keg and all the cups just as a cop raps his nightstick against the glass doors, hand above his eyes, trying to get a look inside. "Hello..."

Mary pauses to compose herself, putting her gum in an ashtray before heading to the front door.

"Open up," says the cop once he spots her.

"Sorry," tries Mary. "We're closed."

"I should hope so." The cop removes his hat. "I'd like to have a word with you."

"Uh, okay, just a sec." Mary looks around, making sure the boys have cleared out, and unlocks the door.

He steps inside. "You the manager?"

"Uh, no, assistant manager." Mary sizes him up; mid-thirties, full head of hair, not a slob, and a thick but well-groomed blond mustache. She reads his badge, thinking a little flirting could get them off the hook. "Though I hope someday, Sergeant Kozlowski, I might earn a promotion."

He doesn't seem too fazed. "Anybody else here?" he asks.

"Just me," steps up Misty, holding a mop.

An older cop, Lieutenant Brady, saunters in the door, his hefty stomach leading the way. "Don't you think it's time to call it a night?"

Misty nods her head. "Yes, sir."

But Mary's curious, not to mention vexed that her drinking game with the boys was so rudely interrupted. "Is there a problem?"

"We've had a few calls," says Brady, positioning himself in front of a fan. "Appears to have been some vandalism in the area."

"Really?" asks Mary, pretending a little too hard that she cares.

"Most likely the usual punks," Brady tells them.

Misty takes the keys from Mary. "We'll be sure to lock up tight."

"That's a good idea." Brady turns and leaves, back to the parking lot. "Goodnight, ladies."

Mary gives the cops a wink and a wave goodbye.

Kozlowski knows Mary's having a laugh at their expense but just puts his hat back on and follows his partner to their squad car, mumbling something to the girls about keeping an eye out.

Misty breathes a sigh of relief and locks the door, looking back at Mary. "The usual punks," she repeats, knowing exactly who that is.

Up on the roof of the Fleetwood, Jack passes a bottle of vodka to Ian, skipping his little brother Joey who looks like he's about to throw up. And then he does ... barely turning his head away.

Ian pushes Joey aside and wipes the lip of the bottle clean with his t-shirt. "I hope it's not contagious."

"Cops're leaving," says Jack, sneaking a look over the edge of the building to the parking lot. "We've lost them."

"Fuck that." Ian launches the bottle at the cop car as it pulls into the street...

And it *smashes,* a *CRACK* of glass and concrete, just shy of the rear fender.

"Why'd you do that?" asks Jack, not really expecting an answer. "We were in the clear."

"Because," replies Ian. "They're still looking for us."

"Stupid punks." Lieutenant Brady reverses course, circling the squad car behind the Fleetwood, where he's certain they've found what they're looking for, a group of teenage boys huddled around a keg of beer.

Sergeant Kozlowski rolls down his window. "Well, look what we have here."

Bobby turns and sees the cops, startled at first, then scared. "Oh, shit."

Kozlowski steps out of the car, serious. "You think it's funny throwing bottles at the police?"

"Uh, no sir," mutters Bobby.

Perhaps Brady expected the boys to make a run for it because he seems annoyed that he has to get out of the car again. He takes a deep breath and stands up, one leg at a time. "You know what I would've done to you had that bottle hit my car?"

Scooter tries the truth. "We have no idea what you're talking about."

"Is that right?" asks Brady. "I suppose you're not standing next to a keg of beer then either."

Kozlowski looks over at Brady for approval. "Some suds might come in handy for softball tomorrow night."

But Brady focuses on the boys. "That bottle could've taken out my tail-light," he says, dreading the thought. "You think I have time for that shit? Well, I don't."

Taking his superior's displeasure as a yes, Kozlowski opens the squad car's trunk. "If you boys don't mind."

Scooter realizes they don't have much of a choice and helps Tim load the keg in the car. "Is that it?" he asks, when they're done.

"Let's talk it over at the station," suggests Brady.

Kozlowski holds the back door open for the boys who reluctantly file in...

When Misty rushes around the corner of the Fleetwood and hugs Bobby goodbye through the window. "Don't worry," she tells him. "We've still got the Ramones concert."

"Actually," says Bobby. "I don't have the tickets just yet. I mean, I did but ... they were kind of stolen."

Misty doesn't get it, or him. "So why'd you even tell me?"

"Because I was hoping I could get them back," he replies. "For you. For us."

Sergeant Brady puts the keys in the ignition. "That's all well and good but you lovebirds are gonna have to figure this out on your own time."

"I'll call you," promises Bobby.

"Maybe you shouldn't." Disappointed, Misty heads back inside the roller rink. "Maybe we're doomed."

Brady hits the gas, driving off with Kozlowski and the boys, unaware they're being serenaded from the roof of the Fleetwood by Ian and Carl, even Joey, singing a hit Steam song from 1969 that's been brought back to life at Comiskey Park.

The White Sox use it to send off their defeated opponents and, tonight, so do the boys from the South Side:

Na Na Na Na
Na Na Na Na
Hey Hey Hey
Goodbye

Chapter 10

SO LONELY

Since Debbie took the Rabbit, and the Mercury was still at the Fleetwood, Bobby and the boys spent the night in a Chicago jail cell with all the other derelicts that got rounded up on a hot Wednesday in July. And though being behind bars on the South Side with a pimp, a professional thief, and a knife-wielding maniac looks decent on a street cred resume', it was a little more than the boys had bargained for when they set out to repair Bobby's love life.

Lieutenant Brady gave them one phone call between the four of them. As a result, the boys deliberated for close to ten minutes. Scooter didn't have anyone to call--who would come. Reggie didn't dare wake up his mother, even with good news. And Tim was hoping to tell his folks he slept at Bobby's house. Then, of course, there was the Mercury to deal with.

Consequently, Bobby's dad bailed them out the next day on his way to work. He took the train in again and took his time. Told his boss he'd be in by lunch, family emergency, though he was quite content to let the boys sweat it out a couple of more hours to make sure they got the point: *Don't mess up*.

And, yes, the boys were pushing it with the keg, but they didn't actually get charged with underage drinking or even possession, since Sergeant Kozlowski kept the beer for the police softball game that night. Of course, their game was interrupted and eventually canceled due the call to arms at another ballgame, the one at 35th and Shields.

The cops wanted them for spray-painting a bunch of garages near the Fleetwood, but obviously none of the boys had any evidence of paint on them or a connection to the graffiti. So they just got them for throwing the bottle, "unintentionally," at the squad car, a court date to be announced.

Bobby's dad is pissed. At least, he's acting pissed. The other parents would expect it of him. Still, there's a long neglected space in his man-soul that's proud of his son for kicking up a little dirt.

He drives the boys home in mock stern silence, until they get about halfway to Evanston, then goes into the obligatory grim routine. "You're lucky they didn't push you on the keg."

"If it isn't breaking and entering," reasons Scooter, "There's no crime."

"Just because you don't break anything on your way in doesn't mean you get a parting gift," counters Bobby's dad, not expecting a rebuttal. Miffed, he looks over at Scooter, sitting opposite him. "Do you just make this shit up as you go along?"

"Why?" asks Scooter. "What does everyone else do?"

"That's funny," says Bobby's dad, thinking just the opposite. "Bobby, I know you weren't drinking and driving."

"I shared one beer with Misty," he says, truthfully. "I don't think we even finished it."

"Tell it to the judge," says his dad, relieved but not letting up on them.

"*Here comes the judge, here comes the judge,*" jokes Scooter, causing the boys in the back to snort and snicker against their will.

"I'll drop you boys off right here in the city," says Bobby's dad, getting angry.

"Relax," Bobby tells him. "It's just a Flip Wilson routine."

"I know who Flip Wilson is," yells his dad. He wanted to go easy on Bobby. But he challenged him. Again, he admires his son's tenacity but not necessarily at his own expense.

After dropping the other boys off at their respective homes, and leaving it up to each of them to tell their parents what happened last night, Bobby's dad orders his wayward son to his room, back to the basement.

Bobby turns on a fan and lays down on his bed, sweating, staring restlessly at his dad's tools, his mind drifting to when Misty first stepped off the boat...

When his mom walks in. "Peanut butter and jelly," she says, setting the plate on his stomach. "Should make you feel better."

Bobby sits up, grateful yet irritated. "I'm not sick."

"Do you want a glass of milk?"

"I can get it," Bobby tells her, starting in on the sandwich. "Thanks."

"Actually, you can't," she informs him. "Your dad said you're to stay put down here today."

"Really?"

"That and you're grounded for the rest of the summer."

"What?" asks a stunned Bobby, between bites.

"He started with the rest of your life so I'd be grateful."

"Grateful?"

"It's my fault," she sighs. "I never should've let you go into the city for your bike."

"It's okay, mom."

"No, it's not. You fell in love, didn't you?"

"Mom..."

"It happens when you least expect it. Just pick a girl from

around here next time." She starts back up the stairs to the kitchen. "Less trouble."

Bobby turns his radio on to the Loop, where Dahl's giving his final broadcast before the big night at Comiskey Park:

```
"The Insane Coho Lips are
dedicated to the eradication and
elimination of the musical disease
known as disco."
```

Bobby picks up his cardboard cutout of Travolta from the floor, like the punch was all a mistake, and asks his idol for advice. "John, my man, what am I supposed to do?"

"Get the girl," says Scooter, walking down the stairs.

"What're you doing here?"

"You don't really talk to that thing, do you?"

"No, not usually."

"I told your mom I was locked out of my apartment."

Bobby hands Scooter half a sandwich. "Did she tell you I'm grounded?"

"Yeah."

"So being stuck in this dungeon makes it kind of hard to *get the girl.*"

"You really want to leave things the way you did with Misty?"

"How'd I leave things?"

"Going to jail. Almost getting her fired from her job. Asking her to a Ramones concert when you don't even have tickets."

"I fixed her boot," says Bobby. "I mean, the guy at Vose did."

"Yeah, that was cool."

"And it was her mom's, which was important to her."

"Very cool."

"But like I said, I'm grounded. There's not much I can do."

"Grounded's perfect."

"How so?"

"Because you're a good little boy." Scooter lights a cigarette. "Your parents will never know you've left."

"No way, I'm already three feet under down here."

"You've got nothing to lose then."

"Um, yeah, another three feet." Bobby shoos the smoke away and shuts the vent to the kitchen. "Makes six in case you weren't counting."

"Come on, it's now or never with Misty."

"And where're we in such a hurry to go?"

"Disco Demolition Night."

"That's right," perks up Bobby.

"You said Misty asked you to go."

"Yeah, but I'm sure she's made other plans by now."

"Who cares?" Scooter lines up a shot on the bumper pool table and casually banks it in. "We'll find her there."

"How?" asks Bobby.

"It's a Sox game," replies Scooter. "How crowded can it get?"

"I don't know, I mean, my parents, sounds risky."

"Dude, Lorelei is going to be at the game." Scooter pats him on the back. "If I can go to the South Side with you to see Misty, you can come with me to see the Loop girl."

"But you don't have a chance with the Loop girl."

"Couldn't be any worse than you're doing with Misty."

"Thanks."

"It's your own fault," says Scooter. "You're the one who went and blabbed to Misty that you had Ramones tickets. Now we have to get them back from Woody."

"So we're going to Beta again?" asks Bobby.

"Obviously."

"You know you're nuts, right?"

"There's a fine line," says Scooter, "between being nuts and having balls."

"I agree and it's too small to wager my life on."

"Don't worry. Just grab a couple of disco records."

"But what about the concert tickets?" asks Bobby.

"I'm working on that." Scooter opens the storm doors, letting in the afternoon light. "Get all the oregano you can from your mom's kitchen cabinet and meet us over at Tim's in an hour." Scooter walks back up the kitchen stairs. "I'll tell your mom you fell asleep on my way out."

Bobby just stands there, watching him leave, his heart already racing across town. "Oregano?"

Half an hour later, Bobby sneaks upstairs to Debbie's room and grabs her Journey concert t-shirt; one from the *Evolution* tour when they played the Aragon in May with Blackfoot (the same show Misty was at). Then, with a backpack over his shoulders and the cardboard Travolta under his arm, he uses the storm doors to slip out of the basement and rides his Stingray down Orrington Avenue and then up towards Ridge before cutting into an alley over by Noyes school...

Bobby pedals right into Tim's garage, where Scooter's waiting for him, already drinking a can of Old Milwaukee. "What's he doing here?" he asks, taking Travolta from him.

"I'm not sure yet." Bobby gets off his bike and leans it against the wall. "I just know that if my parents find out I'm gone, I'm toast. They'll probably send me to one of those creepy prep schools back East."

"Dude, my neighbor on Judson, his parents left him out in the woods for three weeks with some total squares."

"Thanks, that helps..." Bobby hands him the backpack. "*Not.*"

Reggie pulls up in the alley in his dad's Impala. "Why're we doing this again?"

"Why wouldn't we?" Scooter waves Reggie inside the garage and starts in on the backpack, pulling out LPs and 45s one-by-one: "Donna Summer, Chic, The Trammps, Alicia Bridges..."

Reggie gets out of the car. "What time does the first game start?" he asks, hopping over to them on one leg.

"We're on the clock," Scooter tells him. "Bottom of two. I just had it on the radio."

"Is Alicia for me?" jokes Reggie, picking up her record.

"These're our tickets," explains Bobby.

"I know," says Reggie, studying her picture on the cover. "I just don't get why she's wearing a toga?"

"Maybe she just saw *Animal House*." Scooter takes the record back from Reggie and puts it in the backpack with the others.

"What happened to your crutches?" asks Bobby.

"Mother said if my ankle hurt so bad that I had to use crutches, I couldn't go out," replies Reggie. "So I left them, kind of. Got one in the trunk just in case."

"Nice move," says Scooter. "Do you need me to drive?"

"It's my left foot," says Reggie, pointing at it. "You keep drinking the Old Milks."

"Good thinking," concedes Scooter.

Reggie turns to Bobby. "My parents don't know a thing about last night. At least not yet. Thanks."

"No biggie," says Bobby. "Tim's in the clear too. Besides, it was my fault for dragging you guys down there."

Reggie shakes his head. "I can't believe you're giving up your disco records."

"It's all about Misty now," says Bobby.

Reggie admires his friend's fighting spirit but just laughs. "So getting arrested wasn't enough for you?"

"It won't go on our permanent record," interjects Scooter.

"And how would you know?" asks Reggie, before realizing Scooter's probably an expert on such matters.

Bobby pops the trunk on Reggie's Impala and puts his bike and Travolta inside. "We're just going to a baseball game, Reg."

"Let's get out of here," says Tim, hustling out to the alley. "Before my dad changes his mind."

"Where'd you tell him you were going?" asks Bobby.

"Said we were watching the Sox game at your house." Tim pulls a bottle of oregano out from under his shirt and gives it to Scooter. "Of course, he didn't believe me."

"It's the Sox," says Reggie, getting behind the wheel. "Who can blame him?"

Scooter joins him up front. "Anyone else bring some?"

Bobby digs into the bottom of his backpack and hands over the bottle of oregano from his house. "Here."

"Reggie?" tries Scooter.

"I struck out," he says. "My mother was cookin' with it. She puts it on everything, says it keeps her from bloating."

Tim shakes his head, joining Bobby in the backseat. "Um, I'm pretty sure we didn't need to know that."

Less than five minutes later, Reggie parks the Impala in front of the Beta House. "You guys sure you don't want me in there?"

"Not with your ankle," says Scooter, pouring the oregano into two plastic baggies. "Could turn into a footrace again."

"Be careful," Reggie warns them. "Seriously."

"Don't worry, we called ahead this time." Scooter holds up the bags. "By the time Woody figures out what this really is we'll be long gone."

"Let's do this," says Bobby, getting out of the car with Scooter. "Tim?"

"Yeah, okay." Tim follows Scooter and Bobby to the Beta

house, still not convinced that returning to the scene of the crime is such good idea. However, he also understands that it's pointless for Bobby to try and find Misty at Disco Demolition Night without having the Ramones tickets on him. Plus, Tim figures, he can get what he wanted all along, the chance to poke around for his Cub hat.

Fortunately, Beta is pretty much empty tonight, allowing the boys to go straight upstairs to Woody's room.

"It's not locked," he says.

Scooter opens the door to find a girl, a different one from two nights ago, putting her bra back on, giving the boys an unexpected glimpse of her larger than usual breasts.

Tim pushes forward into the tiny room. "Sweet..."

But Bobby keeps his cool, barely. "Sorry."

"That's okay," says Woody, reclining on an over-worked Lazy Boy in just his boxers.

"I was apologizing to her," clarifies Bobby.

"Well, I hope she didn't frighten you." Woody gets up out of the chair and walks the girl to the door, over-doing a kiss goodbye for the benefit of his intruders.

"We get it," says Scooter, interrupting them. "We've seen tits before."

The girl turns her nose up at Scooter and leaves, muttering something to the effect of what he should go do to himself.

Woody forces a laugh. "Maybe one day you'll actually touch a pair, hippie boy."

Scooter knows he should keep his mouth shut. "Hey, I'm not gonna say something stupid like I touched your mom's tits," he says, "but I did lick 'em. Mm-mm good."

Woody takes a swing at Scooter's head...

However, Bobby comes between them, pushing them apart but catching a hard elbow in the jaw for his efforts. "Show him the bag," he tells Scooter, determined to get what he came for.

Scooter hands the bag of oregano over to Woody, who sits back down in his chair to check it out. "Looks okay," he says, "but," taking a sniff, "it smells weird."

"Well..." fumbles Scooter, not expecting Woody to notice the difference.

"Well what?" Woody wants to know.

That's when, out of the blue, Tim steps up. "Well then you obviously know your Thai stick," he says.

"Of course I do," says Woody, too eager to take a compliment. "But there's not much of it."

"That's cause it's so good," Scooter tells him, regaining his footing. "One hit. *See ya.*"

"I don't know," says Woody. "For the Ramones tickets?"

"Yeah, hold on..." Scooter digs through his pockets, remembering his pipe with the last of the real weed. "I packed a bowl, so you can get a taste."

"Gimme that." Woody takes the pipe from Scooter. "The bros want to kill you."

"I can't blame them," starts Bobby, "but I thought we should leave things on good terms." He lights the bowl for him.

"Hmmm," thinks Woody, taking a hit.

"I mean, you did date my sister," continues Bobby. "And this way you get your weed back, better weed actually, and I get my Ramones tickets."

Woody blows his hit out... "I suppose I'll be down in Carbondale when the concert rolls around anyway."

"So do we have a deal?" asks Bobby.

"What about our keg?" wonders Woody. "And the tap?"

"We got busted," Bobby tells him. "Cops have 'em."

Woody shrugs like the deal is off, handing the pipe back to Scooter. "Then our fraternity loses the deposit."

"Crap," moans Bobby.

But Scooter reaches into his pocket for the second bag of oregano and acts like he's totally bummed to have to fork it over to Woody. "You're gonna have to give me enough to roll a joint."

"I don't have to do anything," says Woody, handing the Ramones tickets to Bobby. "Now get the fuck outta here before I change my mind."

"No problem," Bobby tells him, halfway out the door. "It's a beautiful day for a ballgame."

Chapter 11

ROCK 'N' ROLL FANTASY

Reggie drives the boys south on the Dan Ryan into Chicago, mere miles from Comiskey Park. Windows down, radio cranked, and fists pumping, the four of them shout along to the Ramones "Blitzkrieg Bop":

> *HEY HO,*
>
> *LET'S GO!*
>
> *HEY HO,*
>
> *LET'S GO!*

"What a save, Timmer!" yells Bobby, totally stoked.

"That was Tony Esposito quality," adds Scooter, reaching over the seat to slap Tim *five*.

"Sometimes," smiles Tim. "You just tell people what they wanna here."

"And Scooter, putting it in two bags and then busting out the pipe." Bobby pats him on the shoulder. "That was genius."

"Divide and conquer," jokes Scooter.

"He thought he was taking us," says Tim.

"He's gonna shit himself," laughs Bobby, "when he finds out otherwise."

"Oh, man," says Reggie, the first to notice all the brake lights up ahead.

Bobby's worried. "What inning do you think they're in?"

"Must be the seventh by now," replies Scooter. "Maybe the eighth."

"This doesn't look good," says Reggie, bringing the Impala to a complete stop in front of a wall of cars.

"Misty was right." Bobby slumps down in his seat. "We're doomed."

And right on que a sheriff deputy gets out of his car and lights a series of flares, blocking the 35th Street exit to the ballpark.

"How can they close the exit?" wonders Reggie. "Sox Park can't be sold out."

"They're playing the Tigers for fuck's sake," says Tim. "Who do they have except Steve Kemp?"

"Chill, dude." Scooter reaches for the glove compartment. "I've got a couple of beers left."

But Reggie holds his arm out, stopping him. "Not so fast."

"More cops?" asks Bobby, looking around.

"No," replies Reggie, adjusting the side-view mirror to confirm his worst fears. "It's him."

Scooter scans the growing number of cars behind them. "Who's him?" he asks, finding mostly overheated rockers like himself waiting for traffic to get moving toward the ballpark again.

But one guy is making his way on foot...

Tim spots him right away. "It's goddamn Woody."

"Woody?" repeats Scooter. "That can't be good."

"Fuuuuuuck!" howls Bobby. "He's going to kill me."

"Why can't white people leave shit alone?" asks Reggie.

The boys watch in horror as a bloodthirsty Woody darts

through traffic, searching frantically, vehicle after vehicle, for, most likely, *them*.

"Your bike's in the back," says Scooter, getting out of the Impala.

Reggie pops the trunk while Tim and Bobby hustle around to meet Scooter behind the car.

That's when Woody eyeballs his prey, maybe twenty cars ahead of him.

Bobby yanks his Stingray out of the trunk and hops on, pausing only to slip the backpack over his shoulders as Scooter stuffs Travolta, feet first, into the top of the pack so that it looks like Tony Manero is going along for the ride.

"Use the Force," Scooter tells him.

"Get moving!" yells Tim, just as Woody catches up.

Bobby takes off on his bike between the cars, which are situated like a steel maze up the Dan Ryan, turning him left and right and back again...

In the meantime, Tim heads for Woody, blocking him between a Pacer and a Pinto, but Woody plows right through him, punching him in the face for his efforts, leaving Tim clutching his eye as he falls like a tree to the pavement.

Scooter's next in line to keep Woody from going after Bobby, who's pedaling like crazy toward 35th Street...

And just like that, Woody tosses Scooter over the hood of the Impala like a rag-doll, shouting after Bobby, "*Your ass is grass, motherfucker!*"

However, Reggie sneaks up from behind him and hammers Woody over the head with his crutch. "Take that, *sucka!*"

Woody is definitely dazed, his knees even beginning to buckle, when he somehow pulls his shit together and backhands Reggie off his feet.

Woody grabs the crutch and holds it over Reggie, daring him

to get up before he finds Bobby again, not too far ahead, and races after him...

Unfortunately, Bobby's still having trouble picking up any speed due to all the haphazardly stopped cars in his way. Even the side of the road is blocked with cars trying to form their own lane to Comiskey.

Bobby looks back, realizing that at this pace Woody's eventually going to catch up to him. So he gambles and stops, gently laying down his Stingray to face his impending doom.

But first he reaches into his backpack for a disco record. Though, knowing what he's going to do with it, he can't decide which one. Finally, he pulls out the Trammps. Why not? *Disco Inferno*.

With Woody bearing down on him, Bobby takes the album out of its sleeve, all 33-1/3 RPMs, and rears back, winging it at the 19-year-old beast like a frisbee...

Just missing Woody's head, it smashes into the windshield of a '74 Plymouth Barracuda right behind him.

"Sorry!" shouts Bobby to the car crammed full of rockers, who luckily are more amazed than angry.

Screw it, thinks Bobby. He grabs the Alicia Bridges record, the one with "I Love The Nightlife," and flings it at Woody...

Catching him in the thigh, where it cuts through his jeans and momentarily sticks in his flesh.

Still, the gaping wound barely slows Woody down, and he keeps coming for Bobby, the twenty feet or so between them diminishing rapidly.

Bobby tries again with Chic, *C'est Chic* to be precise, but it sails on him... *missing badly*.

Woody's down to ten feet and counting..........

Bobby can see his eyes, glazed with rage. It's me or him, he thinks. So Bobby goes for broke, grabbing both records from the

Saturday Night Fever double album, and promptly lets loose side one...

Woody ducks to avoid it and stumbles, giving Bobby one last chance with side two. "Brothers don't fail me now," he says, snapping his wrist forward and flinging Barry, Robin, and Maurice as hard as he can...

Nailing Woody in the forehead with a resounding THUD. The record doesn't even break. Woody's eyes go cross and he topples over, down for the count. Roger and out. Donesville. And the rockers in the Barracuda cheer loudly.

Psyched, Bobby picks up his Stingray and starts one last time for the ballpark...

When Bobby finally arrives at the monument to brick and steel called Comiskey Park, rockers outnumber baseball fans 50 to 1. Packs of Insane Coho Lips in worn jeans and faded t-shirts, a hint of their first mustache to go with their long summer hair, dart this way and that, desperate to get inside the game.

Thanks to the added attraction of Disco Demolition Night, the ballpark looks like a giant beehive with all its bees hurrying home at once in the last light of the sun. Sensing that the gates are about to shut for the night, a group of older rockers in their twenties begin to scale a drainage pipe on the stadium wall, forming a human chain to get a bunch of total babes in the park.

Bobby realizes he has to act fast if he's going to get in, but he doesn't know what to do with his bike, seeing as he's forgot his padlock. However, Bobby didn't risk life and limb to come all the way down here for nothing. He came for Misty.

So he stashes the Stingray, Travolta too, between a couple of dumpsters outside Comiskey and takes his final disco record, a 45 of Donna Summer's "Last Dance" out of his backpack.

Bobby squeezes through the crowd, finding the shortest line, and reluctantly stands at the end to wait. And wait. But the line barely moves. The park must be close to selling out, thinks Bobby. And if the first game isn't over, it will be soon. He's not sure he's going to make it. And now the cops are telling people to go home.

Desperate times occasionally call for deceiving measures, so Bobby makes his way up to the front of the line and acts like he got left behind, calling out toward the gates. "Dad, wait, I'm not in yet. Dad! Dad! Dad!"

A Sox security guard, a white guy with an impressive beer gut and a walkie-talkie notices Bobby. "What's *yer* problem?" he asks.

"My dad," explains Bobby. "He thought I was right behind him but I bent over to tie my shoe and now he's inside."

"*Yous* got a ticket?"

"I have a buck and this." Bobby shows him the record.

"You can keep the record," he says. "They've stopped collecting 'em." He hands Bobby a poster of Lorelei and lets him pass through the turnstile, pocketing the dollar.

Bobby walks into a jam-packed Comiskey Park for the very first time... And with the temperature still hovering around 80 degrees, the place reeks of beer, weed, and the sweet and sour sweat of youth. Built in 1910 by the founder and owner of the team, Charles Comiskey, it was known as "The Baseball Palace of the World" in its heyday, notable for its giant arched facades that gave fans a view of the neighborhood. It's also where Joe Louis won the heavyweight boxing title in 1937, the Chicago Cardinals won the NFL Championship in 1947, and the Beatles performed to thousands of crazed young fans in 1965.

However, if the Beatles were about screaming girls then Disco Demolition Night is about *yelling* boys. Because they are amped. This is the biggest party a rocker could ever dream of; a show of power, whether you were a hammerhead, a punk, a hippy, or just a regular rocker, it doesn't matter, just that you thought disco was a bunch of bullshit.

Pure and simple: *Toss me a beer. Where's the bong? You up for some ping pong? Put on some Floyd.* This is the rocker lifestyle and tonight at Sox Park, on the twelfth day of July in 1979, this is their town hall, their promised land, their rock 'n' roll fantasy.

The first game is over and the park is swelling, like it's coming apart at the seams, and Bobby can't find a seat. In fact, there's barely enough room to move, so he finally gives up and sits in the aisle, way back in the nosebleed section of the upper deck.

Bobby can't believe all the rockers. I'm never gonna find Misty, he thinks. It's as if every die-hard rock 'n' roll fan under the age of thirty within earshot of Dahl and the Loop has descended upon the ballpark. The coolest of the cool. Then Bobby sees it, a huge green crate containing the thousands of disco records that the rockers came with being brought out to center field.

Comiskey can seat 45,000 fans, though the largest crowd ever to attend a baseball game there was a standing room only 55,000 for a "Bat Day" promotion in 1973. And they've miraculously matched that number today. However, Sox officials aren't prepared for the other 20,000 drunk and stoned rockers who are still trying to get inside—-one way or another.

"This is going to be gnarly," says a young stoner dude to no one in particular, trying not to spill his two beers. He sits down next to Bobby on the steps. "Thirsty?" he asks, already handing Bobby a cup.

"Thanks, I just got here."

The stoner dude takes a big drink of his beer. "Ahh, what I wouldn't do right now for a plate of barbeque ribs."

"Ribs?" asks Bobby. "Now?"

"That was a joke," he tells him, surprised he didn't know the line. "You're not from around here, huh?"

"Evanston," replies Bobby. "How'd you get the beer?"

"My buddy just bought a case of Falstaff off a vendor."

"Cool."

"Yes and no, considering he got mobbed by all our friends-- name's Blaze."

"Bob, Robert, everybody calls me Bobby, I don't know. Nice to meet you."

"Get out much, my man?"

"Not like this, though it's been a crazy week," admits Bobby. He takes a sip, almost getting used to the taste of beer after all the drinking he's done lately. In fact, that Falstaff is going down pretty easy right now. "Check it out." Bobby points to the outfield, past the scoreboard, where teenagers are climbing the chain link fence to get in the game. "They look like spiders from here."

Blaze just smiles, nodding over his shoulder to where hundreds of quick thinking rockers are sneaking into the upper deck from Comiskey's old fire escapes.

"Shit," worries Bobby. "The entire grandstand feels like it's shaking."

"That's 'cause it is," laughs Blaze, pulling out a joint. "Oh man, you should've seen it, the Tiger outfielders were wearing batting helmets during the first game."

"Why?" Bobby gets his lighter out and fires up the joint for his new friend.

Blaze takes a hit and motions to the record that Bobby's clutching under his armpit. "Can I borrow that?" He holds out the joint.

Bobby exchanges the record for the joint and takes a decent hit, then quickly blows it out, watching it join other clouds of pot and nicotine floating aimlessly in the warm night air.

Blaze looks at the picture of Donna Summer and removes the record from its sleeve. "I have to admit she's pretty fine." Then he stands up and wings it, frisbee style, just like Bobby did on the Dan Ryan, only this record soars all the way to the playing field ... landing by third base. "That's why."

"Not bad." Bobby's bummed about the record but understands that tonight will have its casualties.

"Here, gimme your poster," he says. "I'll make a paper plane."

"Uh, Lorelei's for a friend," tries Bobby. "I don't think he got in."

"Right on."

"So who won the first game?"

Blaze takes another hit from the joint. "I'm not sure," he coughs. "You'd have to ask one of the players."

And Blaze keeps coughing as word comes from the Sox public address announcer: "Now ladies and gentlemen, here are Steve Dahl and Lorelei."

A military jeep enters the playing field through the gates in center field with Steve Dahl, dressed in army · fatigues and a combat helmet, waving to the crowd like a conquering hero...

Beside him are Garry Meier and the Loop girl, Lorelei, who looks like a bustier, perhaps even sexier version of Farrah Fawcett. With big blue eyes and bigger blond hair, Lorelei is a total babe, famous throughout Chicagoland for her Loop, "Where Chicago rocks" commercials, in which she lip-syncs to a barrage of rock 'n' roll songs.

Bobby scans the crowd for Misty as the jeep circles the playing field to chants of "Disco Sucks!" while beers get tossed at Dahl affectionately from the upper decks like confetti. Even the occasional M-80 is thrown, exploding just above the heads of the unsuspecting people below them.

"You lookin' for someone?" asks Blaze, handing Bobby the joint again.

"Yeah, my..." Bobby takes another hit. "This chick."

Blaze stands up. "Get a load of that banner." Most of the bedsheets hanging over the ballpark railings say things like, *The Loop* or *Insane Coho Lips* or even *Welcome Home Skylab,* but this one asks, *What Do Linda Lovelace And Disco Have In Common?* Well, considering Lovelace was a porn star...

"Disco Sucks!" continues to thunder throughout the park as the jeep finishes its victory lap around the playing field, eventually letting Dahl and his cohorts out just behind second base, where the disco demolition ceremony is set to take place.

A man in blue jeans and a Sox helmet takes the microphone, "We're here for the biggest anti-disco demolition in the world tonight. My name is Garry Meier. Will you please welcome the supreme commander, Steve Dahl!"

Garry hands the mic over to Dahl, who just screams, "Paaaaartay!" And a party it is with Dahl leading the ruckus crowd, chanting, "Disco Sucks! Disco Sucks!"

Even White Sox organist and Chicago native Nancy Faust gets in on the fun, playing along to the chants. After all, she's right there with the fans in the upper deck.

Dahl speaks into the mic again: "This is now officially the world's largest anti-disco rally!" The rockers roar. "Well listen, we took all the disco records that you brought tonight. We got 'em in a giant box and we're gonna blow 'em up real good." Another even louder roar of approval reverberates throughout the park. Everyone is on their feet, totally jacked, when Dahl signals the pyrotechnic team to get ready and begins the countdown: "One... Two... Three... Boom! Here they go!"

But there's a problem with the fuse, enough time for Bobby to finally spot Misty, and her long red hair, in the lower deck near the Sox dugout.

"There she is!" yells Bobby. "Misty! Misty!"

But it's pointless because there's a *FLASH* in center field as the fuse catches and *BLOWS THE CRATE OF DISCO RECORDS TO SMITHEREENS*, better than anyone expected, filling the air two-hundred feet high with smoke and debris and thousands of shards of vinyl.

Even Dahl is a bit surprised. "That blowed up real good!" he tells the crowd. "Yeah! The Coho Lips win again!"

"What're you waiting for?" asks Blaze. "Go get your girl."

Bobby chugs the rest of his beer and starts for the exit, which isn't easy considering the throngs of rockers in his way who are practically losing their minds over the explosion.

A rocker in the upper deck climbs onto the yellow foul pole in left and shimmies his way down to the field while Dahl sings his signature song, "Do You Think I'm Disco?":

> I like to dance with girls in sleazy dresses
> Lipstick, nail charms, and makeup in excesses
> Buy them a drink and try and get their number
> Usually they are as cold as a cucumber

Not to be out done, a handful of teenagers lower themselves over the outfield wall and jump onto the field, running toward the infield and sliding into second base as Dahl gets into the chorus:

> Do you think I'm disco?
> Am I superficial?
> Lookin' hip's my only goal
> Do you think I'm disco?
> Maybe it's not too late
> To get into rock and roll!

When Dahl finishes the song he takes one last lap around the park in the jeep and then disappears, back through the fence in center field. Meanwhile, White Sox pitcher Ken Kravec goes to the pitcher's mound to warm up with his catcher for the second game, seemingly oblivious to the growing number rockers on the field behind him; at first ten, maybe twenty, then fifty...

However, by the time Bobby reemerges in the lower deck, the floodgates have opened. Bobby can't believe his eyes as thousands of rockers rush the field like they've just won the World Series of Rock. Forget about it, the cops working security for the game are incapable of stopping them. It's a jail break...

A storm of bottle rockets and cherry bombs rain down from the grandstands, while vinyl disco records whiz by from every direction, occasionally hitting and wounding random people.

Soon pandemonium sets in when someone lights a pile of banners in shallow right field, creating a bonfire, rockers dancing around it like something out of *Lord of the Flies*. A young couple rolls around, making out in the on-deck circle. A group of 13-year-old boys share a bottle of whiskey in the Tigers dugout. And two men dig up and run off with homeplate. It's carnage at Comiskey!

Bobby reaches the Sox dugout just in time to see one of the O'Hollearns run onto the field... But he can't find Misty anywhere. He thinks that she's probably already out there with all the other rockers. And, fired-up as he is, Bobby's about to hop over the wall and look for her when Sox owner Bill Veeck takes a microphone out to where homeplate used to be, in the center of what is fast becoming a full-on riot.

"This is Bill Veeck," he says into the mic. "Please clear the park or we'll have to call off the game and close the park. The television cameras are not on you. So please clear the field. Don't spoil the night for everybody else. Please clear the field so the ball fans can see a game. All right, let's clear the field. This is Bill

Veeck. We'll have to forfeit the game if you don't clear the field."

And though Veeck is quite revered in Chicago, the rockers don't budge. They're too busy wreaking havoc on the field; lighting more bonfires, toppling the batting cage, and ripping up the Kentucky Bluegrass to take a piece of the park home with them.

"Holy Cow!" Harry Caray addresses the crowd from up in the broadcast booth, over-looking the field. "Can you hear me out there?"

Harry has been the White Sox announcer since 1971, a larger than life character who loves baseball and calls games like a true fan, sometimes just like them, with a beer in his hand from the bleachers.

So when Harry talks, people listen. "Okay," he starts again. "To make it an absolutely perfect evening, let's say we all regain our seats so we can play baseball again." The rockers whistle and cheer. "Let's go to our seats now. Okay. Come on, let's go. We wanna win a game."

Still, no luck. The rockers are oblivious and, of course, most of them high as kites.

Bobby scans the field from the edge of the stands, searching for the redhead, certain that once she sees him everything will be all right.

Up in the booth, Harry hands the mic over to Mitch Michaels, another Loop disc jockey. "Hey, give us a break and clear the field," he tries. "Back to your seats."

Nancy Faust helps out with her organ, making it into a song: "*Back to your seats. Back to your seats.*" Then Nancy starts playing "Take Me Out To The Ball Game" with Veeck on lead vocals, still in the middle of the mayhem, surrounded by 10,000 or more rockers running amok like lunatics.

The song is a nice touch, and most everyone sings along.

Unfortunately, no one leaves the field, which is basically getting chewed up and spit out. If ever there was a teenage wasteland, this is it!

Back in Evanston, Bobby's dad is watching the whole thing unfold on WSNS TV44, home of White Sox baseball. Harry's broadcast partner Jimmy Piersall, a former player, isn't happy about any of this. "This garbage of demolishing a record has turned into a fiasco."

Eventually, the White Sox decide that they don't want their viewers subjected to or inspired by such bad behavior and cut the television feed, so Bobby's dad flips on the local news to see if he can get an update.

At the ballpark, a new contingent of police arrive on the scene in full-on riot gear, highlighted by their infamous baby blue helmets, a sure sign that they mean business.

The Chicago police department has earned a no-nonsense reputation, forged in the minds, and heads, of the public just a little over ten years earlier during the 1968 Democratic National Convention.

As a result, the police are able to wrangle the rockers back into the stands and clear the field rather quickly (with minimal injuries and only thirty-nine arrests).

Once again, Nancy hits the right note, playing that Steam song she helped make famous to a new generation, "Na Na Hey Hey Kiss Him Goodbye."

And the fans who remained in the stands sing along happily, wanting to see the second game of the doubleheader, with Harry adding a "Play ball!" at the end.

However, Tiger's manager Sparky Anderson isn't having it, insisting to the umpires that conditions are no longer safe to play baseball and demanding the Sox forfeit the second game.

And with that, Veeck returns to the field a final time. "Will you, will you please all keep your rain checks. We will advise you what to do with them once we figure out ourselves. But please keep your rain checks, they will be good for another day."

A heartbroken Bobby files out of Comiskey Park with the rest of the disgruntled crowd, back to the dumpster for his bike--but it's gone. He's lost Misty. He's lost his bike. He's losing his shit! Only Travolta is there for him ... *and his lighter.*

Bobby's dad settles on WLS Channel 7 to try and figure out what the heck is happening at the ballgame. And thankfully, veteran Chicago anchorman Joel Daly reports on a *Riot At Sox Park*:

> "Steve Dahl, his anti-disco night, it got out of hand, the White Sox promotion obviously backfired when the fans, the young ones took the demonstration much too seriously, spilled out of their seats, mobbing the field. Our Rosemarie Gulley is at 35th and Shields with a live report."

Barbara walks in the living room to see what the fuss is about on the TV. "What's happening?"

"Get Bobby up here," he tells his wife. "He'll want to see this."

"I haven't heard a peep out of him," she says. "I'm sure he's fast asleep."

On the TV, Eyewitness News reporter Rosemarie Gulley, fearing for her safety, reports on the still unfolding riot outside the park:

"A local rock radio station had a
promotion out here tonight whereas
they wanted to blow up disco. So
that, the heat and a lot of drugs
and just a very unruly crowd
presented the problem."

"Holy Jesus!" Bobby's dad points at the TV in near shock. "There's ... behind Rosemarie ... that's ... that's our Bobby!"

Even with Heike barking at the TV, Barbara heads back into the kitchen and calls down the basement stairs, "Bobby!"

"Hold on," says Bobby's dad. "What's he doing to Travolta?"

"John Travolta?" asks Barbara, racing back in. She sits down next to her husband on the couch and takes his hand, the two of them watching their son run past the TV screen holding up the cutout of Travolta--*on fire*.

Outside the ballpark, Bobby gets caught up in the moment, releasing all his anger and frustration--and feeling rather good about it. He dances around wildly with Travolta, holding him by the feet, the head engulfed in flames, when a man horse-collars Bobby and throws him in the back of a red Dodge Monaco.

"Dammit," cusses Bobby to himself, when he realizes he's in a Chicago Fire Department car.

"Thank you, will do," says the man getting behind the wheel.

Bobby begrudgingly says, "thanks," and gets a better look at the guy. It's Misty's dad.

And sitting next to him up front is none other than Misty herself, looking sweet in the *Service Crew* jacket. "Hey, Bobby."

Bobby is surprised, relieved, estatic! "Hey."

"I saw your bike by the dumpsters," she tells him, matter-of-factly.

"What?!"

"It's in the trunk."

"Oh, wow, thanks, I never thought I was gonna see it again," he says, leaning over the front seat. "I never thought I was gonna see you again either."

"Me too," smiles Misty.

"Here..." Bobby reaches into his pocket and pulls out the Ramones tickets, handing them over the seat to Misty. So close to her, he tries to kiss her on the cheek, but she turns at the last second and they meet lips instead for a brief heavenly moment before her dad nudges him back down to earth, and the backseat, with his elbow.

He starts the car. "Just so you know, boy--"

"I get it," Bobby tells him, laughing. "You still don't like me."

Misty's dad smiles and turns on the radio, spinning the dial until he finds a song he likes. "Check it out," he tells them. "This is the end of the song."

Funny days in the park,
Every day's the Fourth of July
People reaching, people touching
A real celebration
Waiting for us all
If we want it, really want it
Can you dig it (yes, I can)
And I've been waiting such a long time
--Chicago

He puts the fire siren on for a minute to break free of the traffic, driving the teenagers away from the chaos surrounding Comiskey Park through calmer city streets, north toward Evanston.

A whirl of emotion fills Bobby's heart, and he leans out the window to set it free, yelling at the top of his lungs: *"LONG LIVE*

ROCK!"

Misty turns the rearview mirror around so her dad can't see what's going to happen next and climbs into the backseat, where she promptly smacks Bobby on the back of the head and pulls him inside the car for a long, uninterrupted, kiss....

NOTES

Steve Dahl's radio dialogue was gathered from a TV interview he did with the great Tom Snyder on the *Tomorrow Show with Tom Snyder*.

All the dialogue at Disco Demolition Night (Steve Dahl, Bill Veeck, Harry Caray, Jimmy Piersall, Garry Meier, and Mitch Michaels) was culled from a fantastic documentary called, *Disco Demolition 25th Anniversary: The Real Story* by Teamworks Media and Halftime Productions LLC.

Joel Daly and Rosemarie Gulley's dialogue was taken from Chicago's ABC Channel 7 newscast on July 12, 1979.

The cover art was done with patience and enthusiasm by VB Creative World: Perfection is our Soul and Sole Motto.

ABOUT THE AUTHOR

DOUG E. JONES graduated from UCLA with a degree in English Literature and a minor in Creative Writing.

He has worked overseas in Australia, Japan, and Costa Rica and traveled extensively in Thailand, Nepal, and India, where his first novel, *Nowhere To Goa*, takes place.

Back in the States, he wrote for the hit TV show *Charmed*.

A native of Evanston, Illinois, Doug currently lives in Los Angeles.

You can contact him at dougejones.com.

Made in the USA
San Bernardino, CA
13 March 2018